Loser at Love

A novel
by

L. Harrison

Copyright © 2018 L.HARRISON

ISBN:9781983018183

Any references to historical events, real people, or real places are used fictitiously. Names, characters, and places are products of the author's imagination.

Ecclesiastes 3:1-8 King James Version (KJV)

3 To every thing there is a season, and a time to every purpose under the heaven:

2 A time to be born, and a time to die; a time to plant, and a time to pluck up that which is planted;

3 A time to kill, and a time to heal; a time to break down, and a time to build up;

4 A time to weep, and a time to laugh; a time to mourn, and a time to dance;

5 A time to cast away stones, and a time to gather stones together; a time to embrace, and a time to refrain from embracing;

6 A time to get, and a time to lose; a time to keep, and a time to cast away;

7 A time to rend, and a time to sew; a time to keep silence, and a time to speak;

8 A time to love, and a time to hate; a time of war, and a time of peace.

Mama always said everything happens for a reason…
I remember one time she got laid off her job right before Christmas
well everything happens for a reason
is all she said.
She didn't seem to worry a bit about it.
She acted liked she didn't have a care in the world and I be dam,
the next week she had a better paying job with benefits. I tend to believe that everything does happen for a reason, but lately there was a lot of things happening and I couldn't find no dam reason at all.

CHAPTER 1

As I walked into the waiting room I kept replaying mama's words in my head. I approached the counter where there were two receptionist sitting, one with a belly full of baby.
How could she work in a place like this I thought to myself.
"Do you have an appointment"
The pregnant one said in her broken English as the other one waited on my answer with a fake caring expression on her face.
"Yes I do"
I said and sat in the chair provided.
After filling out some paperwork I was asked to have a seat in the waiting area and someone will call for me shortly.
"Girl you alright"
Tifa asked as she lifted her purse out of the chair she was saving for me.
I knotted my head yes.
"I just cant wait until this is over"

I said and plopped down in the seat.
Tifa was one of my best friends and she
knew exactly what I was going through.
"Freira Burns" the nurse called out in a
medium to low voice that I would not have
heard if I was sitting on the other side of the
room.
I eased up out of my seat and followed the
old short white woman into a room.
She opened the manila folder and looked
over one of the papers I had field out at the
front desk.
"what day was your last menstrual"
she asked along with other questions I had
already answered on the paper.
After all of the questions she weighed me,
took my blood pressure and drew some
blood.
"Come with me"
she said as she lead me to another waiting
area much smaller than the first. There were
only four chairs and two were already taken.
I sat down and tried not to make eye contact

with the other ladies as they tried to do the same. I couldn't help but notice the tears that filled up the young girl eyes when she lowered her head and immediately my eyes filled up with tears of my own heartache.
I wondered what had brought her here in this very cold quiet place. Was it her parents, a boyfriend or just another one of those reasons.
After the old white lady came and got the two ladies one at a time she finally came and got me. She led me into a office that had a large cherry wood desk and nice black leather chairs that looked much more comfortable than the ones in the rest of the building.
"Hello, I'm doctor Shani"
The man sitting on the other side of the cherry wood desk said as he reached out his hand.
"Please have a seat,
I just want to talk to you about the procedure you are having today"

He went on to say.
I sat and listened as he explained to me all that was going to happen and made me sign more papers about liability and stuff like that.
"who's here to drive you home" he asked.
"My best friend Latifa Lee"
I said with the relief I had knowing I didn't have to have my mama all up in my business.
"Do you have any questions" he said
I pressured my brain to come up with something to ask, but I really didn't have any questions all the questions I had, had already been answered.
"No" I said
with a nervous look on my face.
"Well I will see you in a bit" He said taking his eyes off me and looking in the direction of the old white lady who stood in silence.
"Ok Ms. Burns follow me"
the old short white lady said as she opened

the door of the office that was so warm and cozy feeling unlike the rest of the place.
This time she placed me into a room with an exam table, ultrasound machine and silver tray that held objects I was all too familiar with
"ughh" I thought to myself while holding my belly.
" remove all your clothing and jewelry and put on the gown, you can leave on your socks.
I will be back in a minute."
The old white lady said in a light raspy voice.
After changing into the gown and putting all my belongings in the bag, I climbed onto the table and laid back as comfortable as possible.
"knock, knock"
the door started to open and the old white lady was back with the pregnant receptionist.
"Ms. Burns Maria is going to assist me with

your exam ok"
The old White lady said as she caressed my arm.
After the exam I was moved into another room where I was given an IV the old white lady was not there, but Maria was and she explained to me what was going to happen next.
"Your going to get some medicine that's going to help you relax once the procedure is over you will still have the effect of the medicine so don't get out of bed." she said with a concerned look about her.
Dr. Shani walked in with another nurse behind him that I hadn't seen before.
"Maria we're ready" he said as he signaled for her to start the meds she had just told me about.
"count to ten backwards" she told me while she shot some clear liquid through my IV.
Instead of counting I starting praying and before I could say please GOD

I was already knocked out.
When I opened my eyes everything was a blur.
I laid on my back still as a board and scared to move. My stomach felt lighter but very tender inside and out.
When the nurse noticed my eyes open she rushed over in my direction.
"hey sweetie you ok" she said standing over me and looking straight down into my eyes.
I gave her a head shake yes.
"stay lying down for a lil bit longer ok" she said and I nodded yes again.
When she walked away I could here her talking to someone else so I turned my head to get a better view.
I saw the two other ladies from earlier.
"you ready to go home" she asked the younger looking girl while helping her into the wheel chair.
She looked like she couldn't have been no more than fourteen.

She had her street clothes back on and was getting ready to return to the life that had gotten her all the way here.

On her way out she didn't avoid eye contact as much as before although I could still see the pain in her eyes minus the tears.

Once the nurse left the room a woman that I had saw for the first time was coming out of her sinful sleep.

She seemed confused by were she was at for a moment and probably didn't expect to wake up in a room full of other sinful women.

She lifted her feet from the bed and planted them on the floor then used her arms to lift her sore body up.

"awww uh"

she cried out while holding the bottom of her belly and blood gushed out the bottom of her gown onto the cold white floor.

The nurse had returned a second too late.

While the nurse got the disobedient women under control Maria was at my bed with my

bag of clothes and personal items.
"You can get dress" she said
handing me a giant pad and clean pair of
undies.
She rolled me to the restroom and waited
outside the door while I dressed myself then
she took me back into the recovery room,
gave me after care instructions and rolled
me out a side door.
Tifa was standing at the end of the hallway
and started jogging towards us as we got
closer.
Tifa's car was in front of the building and
Maria helped me in.

CHAPTER 2

Three weeks had went by sense the abortion and I was starting to come around.

Tifa had let me spend most of the time with her at her grandmothers house and since it was summer break from school her grandma didn't notice anything out of the normal plus we always stayed at each others houses days at a time.

Tifa and I have been friends since middle school.

We both were seventeen and going into our Senior year of high school.

Tifa was spoiled rotten most people would say.

She had, had her own car since ninth grade. An all white Hyundai.

She decorated everything inside with tweety bird. The seat covers, floor mats, steering wheel cover, mirror and down to the oversized tweety bird stuff animal in the back window.

The only thing that wasn't tweety bird was the must have if you're a gangsta plush dice hangin from the rearview mirror.

"How you feelin girl" Tifa asked as she entered the room with a bowl of captain crunch cereal.

"I'm good, what you eaten on" I asked even though I already knew.

"Captain Crunch, grandma cooking some breakfast too" she said before stuffing her mouth with a spoon full of cereal.

I was glad to hear that. I hadn't been able to eat the past two days and I was ready to tear up some bacon and eggs.

I crawled out of the bed and grabbed my toothbrush out of my Adidas backpack mama always say never leave your toothbrush in a persons bathroom; they will think your trying to move in. Mama has the funniest sayings.

I tried to be quick leaving the room and

getting into the bathroom before Mrs. Lee saw me, but I had to grab a wash cloth out of the hall closet.

As I was leaving the hall closet on my way back towards the bathroom Mrs. Lee hit the corner

"Hey sweetie I'm cooking breakfast, I know you should be hungry, you seemed a lil tired the past few weeks, You alright" she asked

"Yes mam, I'm fine" I said and headed into the bathroom.

I closed the door and immediately started weeping.

"Do she know I was pregnant" I said to myself.

Let mama tell it all the elderly women know when a woman is pregnant even before the woman know she is. Maybe she dreamed of fish or something crazy like that.

I washed the tears from my eyes and brushed my teeth.

"Y'all come eat"

Mrs. Lee yelled out through the house.
I went back into Tifa's room to put my
toothbrush back in my bag and we both left
out the room heading into the kitchen.
"Ma this looks super good"
Tifa said to her grandma as we filled our
plates with bacon, eggs, grits and toast.
"Thank you grandma"
I said and sat at the table.
Mrs. Lee didn't mind me calling her
grandma like I said me and Tifa has been
friends since middle school.
Actually Mrs. Lee liked me more than any
other friends Tifa claim to have.
I was the only one allowed to stay the night.
Mrs. Lee would even buy me stuff if I was
with them when they went shopping and
sometimes Tifa would make sure I was there
if they were going to the mall just so we
could get matching outfits.
My mom kept me up with the style like
everybody else's parents, but Mrs. Lee
spoiled Tifa.

If there was a shirt she liked Mrs. Lee would let her get it in all colors instead of one.
Mrs. Lee retired from the post office ten years ago and was enjoying life
she owned her house on the Westside of Las Vegas and also three good looking cars including Tifa's Hyundai.
Tifa received a social security check for the passing of her father who was Mrs. Lee's only son and Mrs. Lee would give her allowance every week out of that money.
"What yall girls getting into today"
Mrs. Lee said smiling and showing off her two gold teeth
one with the letter L on it.
Mrs. Lee had style about her.
"Nothin grandma, Fre has plans with her mama and I might go to the basketball game tonight".
I didn't have plans with my mama, but Tifa probably said that to get us out of going to the mall.
She knew I was not up for no walking.

"Well you be careful"
Mrs. Lee said to Tifa, while looking at me with curiosity on her face.
After breakfast Mrs. Lee left the house and Tifa and I cleaned the kitchen before getting dress and leaving ourselves.

CHAPTER 3

When I got home mama was still at work and wasn't due home until around six. Mama didn't mind me staying gone as long as she knew where I was at.
I put the load of dirty clothes from my Adidas bag into the washing machine and went into my room.
I laid across my full size bed and began thinking about all I went through over the past weeks.
I tried thinking about any and everything but HIM!
How could I not think about him when a part of him was just torn out of my body. We both knew that's the way it had to be I was only seventeen and had a full life ahead and he was eighteen and just had graduated and on his way to college.
My pager sent a vibration through my ear from under my pillow I looked at the unrecognizable numbers and turned my

pager upside down to get the message I love u.

I picked up the phone and dialed his number, it rang four times and just as I was about to hang up he picked up.

"Hey Fre I been waiting on you to call me" He said with a pause waiting for me to explain why I hadn't called in a couple days.

"You know I was at Tifa's house and didn't want to talk in front of everybody" I said knowing there was no everybody, just her.

"How you doing" he asked

"I guess fine" I responded in a snappy tone.

"Hey we both decide this together if you forgot, I wish it didn't have to be like this." he said

"Yeah I know" I said hoping to change the subject.

"You feel like going to the movies tonight" he said in a uplifting voice.

Throughout our relationship we always did

things together like going to the movies, bowling and hanging out at the arcade.

He wasn't the type of guy who was a shame of having his girl with him everywhere he went and that's what I loved about him.

"Yeah that's cool, what theatre are we going to" I asked

"It don't matter I guess we can decide later, I will pick you up around eight" he said and we ended the call better than we started it which made me feel a lot better.

Mama walked in a lil after six with a bucket of KFC, a few sides and a 2-liter of Pepsi.

"Mani home " mama asked before she could put down the food.

"No his dad hasn't brought him yet" I said.

"How long you been home?" she asked

"Since this morning" I said

"How is Mrs. Lee?

She made any of those banana puddings while you was there" she asked

"Nope"

I said while in search of a wing out of the

KFC bucket.

"Hey I got that new movie Set it off from Block Busters you wanna watch it with me" she said

as she rushed around the house pulling off her work uniform.

"Mama I'm sorry me and Audi are going to the movies tonight"

I said with a playful pout.

She laughed at my playfulness and kissed my forehead.

I could hear the music bumping from the car as he pulled up to the house.

I opened the front door and waited until he was out of his car and almost on the porch.

I went to my room to grab my purse and pager off the bed.

I could hear Audi in the kitchen talking to Mama about the college he was going to.

When I walked in Audi and mama were studying the cover of the Set it Off movie case.

"You ready" I said interrupting there focal

point.

"Yes…

Bye Mrs. Burns" he said

as he gave her a hug.

"Bye mama" I said while doing the same.

We pulled up to the movie theatre in Audi's dad black Cadillac bumping the new 112 CD.

Although it was Audi's dad car everyone knew who was in it.

He had the car every weekend since I'd known him.

By the time we paid and got into the movie it had already started.

That was fine with us we didn't have to sit through all the previews.

The theatre was packed as usual on a Friday night.

We didn't care about being last to get in the movie, but didn't want to be last getting out cause you know most of the time it was going to be some tripping with all the gang bangers.

After the movie I saw Tifa sitting on the
back of her car with the home girl Lacy.
When she spotted me she ran over arms
opened wide and hugged my neck.
"Hey Bitch" she said
in a playful way as we shared a laugh
together.
"Yeah bitch
were you been hiding at I paged you a
couple times and you didn't call me back."
said Lacy
with a big grin on her face.
We all were closes friends growing up
together and spending almost everyday with
each other.
We told each other everything, but I didn't
want to tell Lacy about the abortion.
"Girl I been spending time with my boo,
you know he leaving soon" I said
in a sad voice.
Just as we were getting off the subject Audi
came walking up.
"What's up? Tifa, Lacy" he said

looking at them then me as if he knew we were talking about him.

"hey Audi"

they both said in unison.

Audi liked Tifa, he even called her his play sister sometimes, but he didn't care for Lacy. He never said it himself, but I knew he didn't like her.

"You ready Fre" Audi said

as he held on to my waist and started walking me into the direction of the all black caddi.

"Bye yall" I said

with my back turned to them as I continued to walk towards the car.

Audi and I ended up at his house with Taco bell.

I had a Mexican pizza with sour cream and he had four taco supreme' s and cinnamon twist.

After eating our food we crashed in the middle of the floor.

When I woke up it was 7a.m.

I looked over at Audi who was sleeping like a baby
"Audi…Audi" I said
as I shook his arm trying to wake him.
"Can you take me home before your dad wakes up for work." I asked.
Knowing his parent would be mad if they knew I had stayed the night without there permission.
Audi's parents liked me and they knew we were sexually active, but they weren't having no shacking up in their house.
If we stayed out late and I had to stay over I would sleep in the guest room which was on the bottom level of the house and all the other bedrooms were on the second floor.
On the drive home I sat quietly listening to the music as he had to be the back up singer for 112
"*cupid*
   never lies,
but you wont know unless you give it a try"
he sung out through his nose.

I laughed inside every time he sung the line because he thought deep down inside he could sing as good as the group.

"What you doing for your birthday"

I said noticing the already opened envelope sitting in the middle console.

His birthday wasn't until next Wednesday the day after he leaves for college so who would give a birthday card this early

I thought to myself, but not sharing my curiosity.

"my mom and dad takin me out" he said and continued with his next line of the song he had blasting through the speakers of the caddi.

"O when"

I asked already knowing he would be in Arizona on his birthday.

"Sunday" he said

as he closed his eyes and finished off the highest note in the song. While I waited on my verbal invitation to dinner with he and his family we had arrived at my house.

We silently stared each other down for a brief moment then he reached his head over to mine and planted a kiss on my lips.

CHAPTER 4

When I walked in the house mama was
getting ready for work and Mani was headed
out the door on his way to his dads house.
"Hi,
Bye
sissy" he said
as he closed the front door before I could
respond.
"How was the movie" I asked mama.
"Girl it was good,
you know I cried,
It's not due back until tomorrow if you want
to watch it" she said.
After mama left for work I went into my
room and started folding the load of clothes
I left in the dryer the day before.
Then I took a warm shower made a bowl of
top ramen noodles and popped the movie
inside my VCR.
Half way through the movie I got a page
from the home girl Lacy so I picked up the

phone receiver and dialed her number.
"Hey bitch what's up" she said
before saying hello.
She already knew it was me because she had
caller ID.
"Hey girl I'm just chillin…
watching this movie Set it off" I said with
excitement in my voice.
She already had seen it so we shared bits
and pieces about the parts of the movie we
liked and how we thought the girls were
soldiers for robbing those banks.
I was still in the middle of the movie when
Lacy blurted out *"all the bitches die"*
"Bitch bye" I said
and hung up the phone.
I continued watching the movie and by the
end I had shedded a tear or two.
I picked up my phone and dialed Tifa's
number and got a busy tone, she must be on
the phone I thought to myself.
Just as I was dialing her again I could hear a
voice through my receiver

"Fre,
Fre" she was calling my name
"hey girl I was just trying to call you" I said.
"I must have been trying to call you at the same time,
what's up" she said.
"girl just got done watching Set it Off, that shit was tight" I said
as I went on and on about the movie, but not giving up too many details.
After I finished with the reason I called her, she started with the reason she was calling me.
"You know Bomb and them having a house party Saturday…
you riding with me RIGHT"
she told rather than asked me.
Bomb was a lil banger that lived in the same projects as Lacy.
He was around our age, but didn't go to our school.
Tifa was in love with his older brother Deuces.

Deuces had to be about three years older than us, but she didn't care.
She knew he would be at the party.
Tifa always claimed Bomb liked me, but I wasn't trying to hear that.
Not because he wasn't cute;
as a matter of fact he was be awn cute he was sexy as hell.
He had smooth dark brown skin with the darkest black eyes the kind you stared at and could easily get lost into if your not careful.
He had jet black hair that you rarely got to see because he always wore a hat.
"YEAH GIRL" I said
with thoughts of what I was going to wear circling in my head.
"Me and Lacy going to the Boulevard Mall to get something to wear to the party, I will pick you up on the way"
she said
knowing that I wanted to go
I didn't mind her telling me instead of asking me.

The only way you was getting to the Boulevard mall is if you had a car so thank God Tifa had a car or else we would be catching the 214 bus to the Meadows Mall and it didn't have nearly as many stores as the Boulevard Mall.

On our way to the mall Lacy asked Tifa to stop so she could pay her beeper bill.

Tifa didn't mind since it was right by the mall anyway.

When we pulled into the mall parking lot I saw Audi's dad Caddi, I knew it was his from the personalized plates.

The girls and I went inside Foot Locker first because we liked to buy our shoes before our outfits.

Tifa and I bought the new High top Grant Hills and Lacy bought all white shell toe Adidas.

We all found matching Guess outfits in Dillard's, but Lacy got her outfit in black and white and me and Tifa got ours in red and white.

After leaving Dillard's we took our usual
stroll around the mall looking in our favorite
stores and flirting with cute boys.
"lets go to the food court before we leave.
I'm dying for a cinnabun right now" I said.
Tifa hooked me on to cinnabuns the first
time she brought me to the boulevard mall.
Now I can't leave without having one.
"I want an Orange Julius" she said
with a big smile.
As we were standing in the line for the
Orange Julius I felt a hand on my
butt and knew it could only be Audi brave
enough to lay a finger on this ass.
I turned around with a smile across my face
"hey Fre what you doing up here" he said
smiling just as hard as I was.
I stepped out of line since I wasn't the one
getting a OJ anyway
"what u got in that bag"
he said grabbing on the bag playfully.
"I bought me an outfit" I said
as I started walking toward the cinnabun

line. We sat four tables away from Tifa and Lacy who ended up getting some Big Mac's and fries to go along with there OJ's.

"So you leaving next week huh" I said answering my own question.

"yep" he said

smiling as hard as his mouth would let him. Tifa and Lacy walked over to let me know they were leaving and to see if I was riding back with them or Audi.

Audi said he would take me home and I waved the girls goodbye as they disappeared in the crowd of people.

Audi and I sat there a lil while longer reminiscing about our pass few years together.

We laughed about our Sadi Hawkins pictures

and he told me how everyone at his school was amazed by how pretty I was

and how all the girls were jealous to know a younger girl had the heart of Audi Tate. That was the first time I had met any of his class mates, but he knew a lot of people that went to my school just from hanging out. The one person from his school I did know was Samantha and if I had saw that bitch there, it would have been a problem.

Audi had cheated on me with Samantha at the beginning of our relationship and what made it so bad, I had to find out through Lacy who said her cousin Mike heard about it from his girlfriend who was Samantha's cousin.

The only reason Mike told Lacy was cause he liked me.

I was happy to know the info, but wasn't happy that it had to come from Lacy.

Lacy was the type of girl who didn't take no shit, when she caught her boyfriend cheating she first whooped the girls ass then his. The next day she started going out with his homeboy from the block.

She thought I should have taught Audi a lesson for cheating.

After I finished the cinnabun Audi and I

stopped in a store looking for white jean shorts to match his white and tan striped shirt.

He went crazy over some all white Lug boots that were on display in the front of the store.

After all his hype over the boots went down he asked the employee for a size 32 in the white jean shorts hanging on the wall.

Before ringing him up at the register she tried selling him a second pair for half off.

That store always offered two for one type of deals, around Christmas time they had a lot of buy one get one free.

He took the deal and ended up with a Tan pair of shorts too.

We left the mall around 5pm and it was 110° outside, that was a typical hot summer day in Vegas.

On the way home we took our usual cruz through the town bumping loud music with so much base it shook the windows of the duplex apartments we passed, I think the kids at the Boys and girls club heard us coming cause when we hit the corner all eyes where on us.

Mama was pulling in the drive way as we pulled up to the house.

We met her at her car to help with the bags she had loaded down in the back of the Durango.

We all waved at Mrs. Rice the next door neighbor before going into the house.

Mrs. Rice spend most of her days sitting out on her porch waiting to see what she can see.

After Audi and I helped mama with the bags he gave me the usual hug and kiss on the cheek before leaving.

"Did you watch the movie" mama said with excitement in her voice.

"Yep it was good too." I said With just as more excitement than her.

"sad ending though" I added with the instant thought in my head of how they did Cleo.

"So when is Audi leaving" she asked
changing the subject faster than it started.
"He said next week"I sadly responded.
Then she started her motherly lecture I
didn't want to hear.
"You need to stop worrying about these
nappy headed boys and focus on school
cause all they thinking about is sex.
Then when you give it up they on to the next
girl and you'll be somewhere pregnant"
she said with an attitude as if I wasn't
listening to a word she said.
"If you know like I know you shouldn't be
thinking about no love.
Just enjoy being young and having fun.
Just to let you know,
nobody ever marry there first love"
she added with a convincing smile.
I was listening to what mama was saying
and I know she knew first hand cause her
and my pops where high school sweethearts.
Mama didn't graduate cause she was
pregnant with me and all she ended up with

was a maid job at the casino.
Pops did graduate and after graduation he
went off to college. Less than a month later
he wanted to date other people.
So maybe mama was right,
maybe I should just wait on love,
be young and have fun.
I grabbed the Footlocker and Dillard's bag
off the kitchen table and headed to my room.
I took the shoes out of the box for a second
fitting, looking at my feet through the big
mirror propped up on the floor
"these too cute" I said aloud.
Mani came walking in my room
"hey sissy those tight"he said
looking down at my new shoes.
Mani loved shoes the way I did, I guess he
got it from me.
Mama use to not buy him expensive shoes
until he got in junior high school and I
begged her not to send him to school in
Power Rangers.
"Me and mama going to the carnival, you

going" he said
shaking his head yes.
I laughed and said yes boo boo,
taking the smile right off his face.
That was mama's nickname for Mani and he
hated it with a passion.
We got to the Field were they had the
carnival set up and found a pretty good park
for it to have been so packed.
Mama bought us all wristbands so we could
ride whatever we wanted to, as many times
as we wanted.
There were a few rides I wouldn't get on
because my stomach still felt a little weird
from the abortion, but of course I blamed it
on just being scared of the ride.
By the end of the night Mani had rode each
ride at least three times if not more.
Mama played the Quarter toss game ten
times trying to win Mani a glow in the dark
football.
On the last try she won it, he was happy.
The drive home was quiet; Mani was sleep,

Mama was grooving to her oldies music she had playing in the CD player and I was thinking about Audi and what was going to happen with our relationship.

CHAPTER 5

I woke up to the vibration of my pager in my ear, I had a habit of sleeping with it under my pillow like most teens.
I saw that Tifa had paged me six times and it was only 9a.m.
I picked up the receiver to dial her number and as usual she was already on the other end.
"Dang girl you must been sitting by the clock" I said
joking because she knew my mama didn't like me getting calls before 9a.m.
"you know what today is"
she said with hype in her voice.
Bomb and them party, I thought in my head
"yes I know,
what time u picking me up" I asked
with fake excitement.
"Be there at six" she said
and we ended the call.
The party didn't start until eight, but we

knew it wouldn't be jumping until about nine or ten so we had plenty of time to get cute and floss around the projects.

I found Mama in the kitchen cooking breakfast and listening to her oldie but goodie CD

"And I cried,
I cri-I-I-I-ied
oh oh oh"

she sang while flipping over the pancake. Mama had the weekends off of work so she spend her off days cleaning house, doing laundry and shopping.

I sometimes bugged her about getting a boyfriend to take her to a movie or out to dinner once in a while, but she claimed she was fine without a man. Since her and Mani's dad break up she didn't have the time for a man.

So she said.

If you ask me I think they'll be back together.

The day went by before I knew it and it was

already five o'clock.

I told mama I was going to a party with Tifa and Lacy and that I will be staying the night at Tifa's.

Mama wasn't like some parents, over protective.

She was the type that would worn you once, tell you twice and then its on you.

I packed my adidas bag with pajama's, extra clothes and my personal hygiene's.

I took my shower and started getting dress.

After being fully dress I walked over to the big mirror and looked myself over front to back.

Just as I was picking up the phone receiver to call Audi, Tifa was honking her horn.

I will page him from Tifa's

I thought to myself as I grabbed my Adidas bag, purse and pager.

I told mama I was leaving and ran out the door.

When we got to Tifa's house her grandma was gone to Jerry's Nugget for the six o'clock Bingo session.

Good for us because that gave us the chance to talk freely as we bump the new Missy Elliott CD throughout the house.

"I cant wait to see Deuces" Tifa said before licking her lips and tracing a black line around them with the eyeliner pencil.

I knew she liked Deuces a lot, but I didn't know why.

She hadn't spend time with him or hadn't even had a conversation for that matter.

She claims he saw her in the corner store and said hey cutie.

Since that day she been in love with her some Deuces.

Tifa didn't have a main boyfriend she just fooled around with a few dudes around the way, but I knew if she could have it her way Deuces would be hers.

"I cant wait either"

I said smiling at her through the bathroom mirror.

I went into Tifa's room and decided to call

Audi from her phone.

After the fifth ring I got the answering machine and left a message.

I laid across Tifa's bed and watched a rerun of 106 and park while she finished her make-up.

We left Tifa's house around seven and it felt good outside, the sun had started to go down and the street lights had started to come on.

We rode through every neighborhood bumping the Missy Elliott CD that we hadn't had a chance to really get to listen to at the house.

We pulled into the gas station for gas, gum and fountain soda's.

Tifa's pager went off as she was pumping the regular unleaded in her gas tank.

"this Lacy" she yelled tapping on the car window to get my attention.

After pumping the gas she pulled the car around to the side of the store where the pay phones were.

"You got a Quarter" she asked
as she looked around the floor of her car.
"Yeah I got one" I said
and opened the car door.
We got Lacy on the phone and arranged to
meet her at her house which was in the same
projects as the party was.
When we got to Lacy's house her mama and
auntie was sitting on the porch drinking beer
and watching the three little kids who were
having a good time getting wet with the
water hose.
"y'all must be going to that party,
Lacy up there"she said
with a drunk smile, reaching for the tall can
of Old English beer that was hiding behind
the leg of the plastic green chair she was
sitting in.
"what party"
the auntie said
as if she was surprised she didn't already
know about it.
"Lois boys"

was all Lacy's mama said in responds to her sisters question and they left it at that.

When we walked in the house it smelled of dirty diapers, fish and funk all mixed together.

We walked up the pitch black flight of stairs reaching a dimly lit hallway. We stepped over the pile of clothes that were blocking the top of the stairway and hurried pass the open room door where we could see a man sitting on a loveseat watching a rerun of the Jerry Springer Show on a floor model T.V. When we got to Lacy's door I obeyed the sign and knocked.

Looking around you could tell Lacy's mom didn't have a regular house cleaning day. There was a pile of trash taking up a corner of the filthy wall next to the bathroom.

"Hey y'all I'm ready"

Lacy said when she opened the door.

Me and Tifa walked into her room closing the door behind us and took a seat on the full size bed that was centered in the middle of room.

Lacy's room was not like the rest of the house, it was clean.

She had made over her room earlier that year with the money one of her aunties had giving her when she carried her on her income taxes.

She painted the walls yellow, bought a 5 piece bedroom set, new curtains and comforter set for her bed.

"We look cute, they gone be hatin" she said spraying her arm and neck with the Bath and Body works body spray.

She handed me the bottle then rubbed her palms together.

"bet not nobody step on the new Grant's either" I said spraying myself and then setting the almost empty bottle on the nightstand.

Me and Tifa headed back through the filthy hallway, down the stairs and back to the front porch were Lacy's mama and auntie where still sitting and drinking there beer.

Lacy came down a little bit after us with her black leather Guess purse in one hand and a disposable camera in the other.
"OOH LOOK AT YALL…
YALL LOOK CUTE ALL DRESSED ALIKE AND STUFF"
Lacy mom said
when she saw Lacy wearing the same outfit as me and Tifa.
"Here take a picture of us" Lacy said tossing the camera in her moms lap.
Her mom stood up from the chair with her belly hanging from the bottom of the Pink Panther pajama top.
She sat the tall can of Old English back behind the leg of the chair and started taking pictures of us.

CHAPTER 6

It was 8:45 p.m. when we started walking towards the back of the projects were Bomb and them lived picking up a few more complements on the way. When we got to the party there were a group of dudes hanging in front of the door watching who enters the apartment.
Inside it was dark and the only light came from a red bulb placed in the hallway. They had Snoop Dogg bumping from the large floor speakers that were placed on each side of a black leather couch.
We walked through the dancing crowd of teens, giving daps to the ones we were cool with and slightly exchanging mad dogs to the ones we weren't.
I followed Tifa and Lacy into the kitchen where they had a punch bowl full of red juice with fruit cocktail inside.
Tifa filled up three Styrofoam cups taking one and leaving the other two for me and

Lacy to grab.

This was not our first house party so we already knew the punch was spiked with alcohol.

Me and Lacy grabbed our drinks and followed behind Tifa back into the living room.

The crowd swayed back and forth as they sung in unison

"Make Em Say Uhh"

"uhh"

"na naw na naw"

By Master P.

Drink in my right hand I raised my left hand as I swayed my body back and forth singing along with the music. Tifa and Lacy not too long after joined me in the lyrics we knew by heart and as the hook came back around we got louder

"Make Em Say Uhh"

"uhh"

"na naw na naw"

We shouted out as we moved closer to the

middle of the floor.

Three songs later and the party was deep. People were damn near back to back and you couldn't hardly see be awn the dance floor.

Lacy and Tifa started a battle with these two hood rats from around the way.

The floor turned into a battling ground as people started forming a circle and giving the girls enough space to show what they had.

Lacy always won the dancing battles all it took was her dropping down into the splits and perculating to the beat of whatever song that was backing her up.

After the battle the crowd gave Lacy madd props and the circle of empty space filled back up with people ready to get there groove on.

Me and the girls went into the kitchen to fill our cups back up with the spiked punch. They played one of Tifa's favorite songs so she handed me her cup and went back to the dance floor.

A short time later she came running in the kitchen with excitement on her face, her body mimicked a baby that couldn't talk, but was trying to say something.

"what,

What is it" I asked

as I waited for her to gather her composer and spit it out.

"Deuces is here" She said

grabbing me by the hand and leading me back into the living room.

We ended up passing right by him as we worked our way across the dance floor to an empty space on the wall.

We watched as Bomb, Deuces and Hip greeted there homies with handshakes and threw up there set to the homies who were standing farther away.

2 Pac Started to play and everybody went crazy.

Bomb and Hip started there gangsta dance together as they sung the lyrics to the song.

You could tell they pre planned there grand entrance which was cool because it did hype the party up even more.
Deuces chopped it up with a few more of his homies and walked towards the hall, disappearing into one of the bedrooms.
"Did you see him girl" Tifa said smiling hard with her fist balled up and body shaking as if she was having an orgasm standing up.
"yeah I seen um" I said as I looked around the room at the new faces that had showed up to the party.
"I wonder why every time they have a party he in the room"
She went on to say,
but this time it seemed as if she was asking herself the question.
It was true though Deuces never stayed out and partied.
If you seen him he would be coming or going.
I don't know why Tifa liked him so much

and she didn't even know him like that.
I don't even think they have ever had a conversation together, but that's her boo she claimed.
"I'm going to the bathroom, I'll be right back" She said
and walked off.
I continued to look around the room trying to see who I could see when Lacy came and pulled me out on the dance floor.
We started shaking our butts to a Lil Kim song.
We even started to do the dance moves from the music video.
I was all into the song and popping my booty when my eyes connected with Bombs. He was standing next to one of the big loud speakers talking to DJ who was sitting on the edge of the black leather sofa. He had a stack of CD's in his left hand and the one he must have wanted to hear in his right. With his eyes still glued on me he handed the single CD over to DJ.

I kept up my dance routine making sure I didn't miss a beat as he kept watching.

After the song ended I searched through the crowd looking for my girls and that's when the house went dark and *R. Kelly, Hey Mr. DJ* came busting through the speakers.

Bitches started grabbing their niggas, niggas started grabbing bitches because it was time to get there freak on.

Not really being able to see I backed myself up until I could feel my back against the wall.

West stood in front of me rolling his body and lip singing to the song

So I started rolling my body as I stepped away from the wall getting closer to him.

"Sis who you here with" He said with a grin on his face

"Tifa and Lacy, boy you already know" I said laughing to myself.

West was in love with him some Lacy, but the home girl wouldn't give him no play.

She said he wasn't her type.
West was a lil more mellower than what she dealt with.
He wasn't the finest with his Chinese eyes and big forehead, but he could out dress any nigga on his worst day.
"Man what's up with Lacy, she be tripping" He said with a big smile on his face.
We both had a laugh and continued our slow dance.
Bomb happened to be a few feet away locked up with some girl slow dancing as well.
With his partners back facing me and my partners back facing him,
We locked eyes again and moved to the same rhythm of the song as if we were grooving together instead of who we were dancing with.
Neither one of us would look away as if we were in a starring contest
And that's when it happened
I had gotten myself lost in his eyes.

Then thankfully someone flicked the switch back on and the red light rescued me.

As the party started to die down I looked around for Tifa who I hadn't seen since she walked off to the bathroom.

I found Lacy by the punch bowl getting her last refill before we had to bounce.

You seen Tifa I said with an inpatient tone to my voice.

Just as we were about to go searching for her, she appeared right in front of us happy as a lark.

"Bitch were you been"

I said in a playful but serious way and really curious to know.

"GIRRRL"

She said as she tried holding in her laughter, excitement and whatever else that seemed to have her so Getty.

"I'll tell y'all later"

She said when she saw ear hustlers close by.

After the party we decided to stay at Lacy's house.

During that night we found out what Tifa was doing while we were shaking our butts and had to hear about it all night.

From what she say, she bumped into Deuces coming out the bathroom as she was going in.

She apologized for being in his way and he said *it's all good.*

On her way out the bathroom she had to pass by the room that he was in and the door was open.

She saw he was the only one in there so she stuck her head in the door and asked him why he wasn't at the party.

He said he was handling some business and was looking through his pager.

She saw that the new R. Kelly video was on BET so she went all the way in the room and continued watching it with him.

He said she can sit down on his bed if she wanted too so she did.

Then she said he asked her if she was the girl who drove the white Hyundai.

She said all they did was talked some more and before she left they exchanged pager numbers.

I was happy that she finally got to talk to Deuces and was wondering where it would go from there, but I also wondering about my own relationship and where it was going.

CHAPTER 7

Soon as I walked through the front door I could hear my phone ringing.

I hurried in my room trying to catch the call before I missed it.

"hello"

"hello" I yelled out into the receiver.

There was no response. I went through the caller ID to see who called and to check if anybody else called while I was gone.

I had a couple of missed calls from my cousin, but none from Audi and whoever had just called had a private number.

After checking the caller ID I dialed Audi's number.

I let the phone ring over six times before I hung up and paged him.

I kicked off my shoes and laid across my bed waiting to see if he would call me.

After waiting nearly an hour for my phone to ring it finally did.

"dang it show take a lot to catch up with

you" I said
before even saying hello.
"you cant call nobody" I said
with the biggest attitude I could possibly
have.
"wasn't you at a party"
Audi responded sarcastically
"what the hell that suppose to mean"
"I called you from Tifa house before I went
to the party and you didn't answer"
I said with anger.
"well I was busy" he said with a little anger
of his own.
After sitting on the phone nearly an hour
trying to sort out our differences he decided
to come over.
By the time he arrived both of our attitudes
were in check.
Since mama wasn't home we cuddled in the
living room and not too long after ended up
in my bedroom.
Mama didn't allow boys at the house less
alone in my room while she was gone and if

she was there bet not no doors be close.
I respected mama's wishes WHEN SHE
WAS THERE, but she wasn't.
Audi laid across the bed on his back and I
climbed on top of him laying my head on his
chest.
"I cant believe I'm leaving in two days"
  he said with less excitement than he had in
the days prior.
"I know" I said with sadness
Audi lifted his body and turned until we
both were laying on our sides facing each
other.
"I'm gonna miss you"
he said to me with the saddest look I had
ever seen from him.
He kissed me on my lips and used his hand
to caress my breast. He rolled over on top of
me and lifted my shirt fully exposing me.
He circled around my nipple with his cold
tongue and then placed my whole breast in
the warmth of his mouth.
He knew we couldn't have sex because of

the abortion and Dr. Shani warned me not to for at least six weeks.

That wasn't the only thing we had to worry about, mama could pop up at any minute and I didn't want to be caught off guard.

We returned to the living room so in case mama did come home she wouldn't be tripping.

"what time is dinner" I said still waiting for my verbal invite

"eight" he said and again left it at that.

I couldn't understand why he was acting so different. One moment happy, next moment sad.

Did it really have something to do with him leaving or was it much more.

Whatever it was I needed to know.

Audi had been long gone by the time mama came home.

"hey honey" she said catching me off guard while I was in a deep train of thought.

"hey mama" I said

as I raised my body from the couch and

headed in the direction of my room.
"what's wrong with you" she asked
with authority.
I was her oldest child and she knew when
something was bothering me.
"nothing" I said
and kept walking.
I was hoping she didn't follow up behind me
pressing the issue and surprisingly she
didn't.
I caught the pager just as it was about to
vibrate it self off the dresser.
My phone started ringing just as I was about
to check my pager.
It was Tifa.
"hello" I said
with a tone she wasn't use to hearing from
me.
"hey girl I just paged you, what's wrong
with you"
She said concerned about her friend.
"nothing" I said,
but just like mama she knew I was lying.

"well I was calling to see if you wanted to hangout with us at Lacy's house" she asked waiting for my answer.
"nall I'm good" I said waiting for her next question.
"Fre what's wrong and don't say nothing cause I know something wrong,
you just not saying"
She said with attitude.
She was right, she knew when something was wrong with me just like I knew when something was wrong with her.
I hated lying like everything was ok, but actually up until a month ago everything was ok
then I ended up pregnant, had an abortion, my man leaving for college in another state and on top of all that I'm dealing with his sudden mood swings.
"look girl we best friends and we go way back,
don't act like I don't know you by now" she said a little more calmer than before.

I wanted to talk, but didn't know what to say so I continued with my lie.
"nothing" I said
again hoping she was ready to leave it alone.
"well I'm coming over" she said
and hung up the phone.
When Tifa got there she seemed sad for me, but I could tell she was happy for another reason.
"why you so happy" I asked
taking the focus off my problem.
She gave me one of her big smiles and said nothing much.
I knew it was something she was hella happy about, but I knew she didn't want to show her happiness while I was sad.
"girl Audi pissing me off"I said
before she had to work on prying the problem out of me.
"what the fuck he do" She asked hyped up
"he just been acting hella funny lately.
I don't know if it has something to do with the abortion or him leaving for school, but

he acting different"
I said shaking my head.
"well shit he the one got you pregnant so
how he gone be mad at that"
She said with anger.
That was true Audi did get me pregnant.
We actually talked about having a baby and
living together after high school, but all that
changed when he got the acceptance letter to
a college in Arizona.
After that we both knew I had to have an
abortion because he would never want to be
a father and not be there to see the baby
grow,
Inside and outside of me.
I thought about keeping the baby, but I also
didn't want to end up like my mother; a
single parent.
"yeah you right" I said
hoping we could end the conversation now
that I had gotten a little bit off my chest, but
Tifa kept going with rage.
"that lil ugly ass nigga know he messing

with the wrong bitch, don't nobody mess with my sista" she continued on and on.

After I finally got her calmed down over my problems I asked her why the hell she was so happy when she got there.

That put the smile right back on her face as she sat down on the bed and started telling her story.

"Girl you know I talked to Deuces today" she said without breaking her smile.

"O what y'all talk about" I asked although I knew she would get to that part next.

Then she went on telling me how she paged him and he called right back unlike the dudes she usually talk to. She said he just asked her what was up with her and what she was doing. She told him she was going to Lacy's house later and might see him around.

"Do he have a girlfriend" I asked as if she cared, but I knew she didn't.

This wouldn't be the first time she messed around with another girls man.

"Don't know, don't care" she quickly replied.

We spent the next thirty minutes just talking about our lives as they stood at that moment.

"You coming to Lacy house" she asked raising up from the bed.

"Naw girl I'ma chill" I said with my thoughts back on Audi.

It was almost nine o'clock and I knew he would be back from dinner soon.

"OK" she said and started walking toward the door.

It was eleven thirty and I still hadn't heard a word from Audi.

I called his house and paged him until I fell asleep.

When I woke up the next morning the phone was off the hook laying on my pillow. I instantly got heated and slammed the phone back on the hook.

I didn't waste time calling him again instead

I called Tifa.

Tifa answered her phone on the first ring.

"Come get me" I said with anger

"What din happen now" she said knowing it had something to do with Audi.

"He playing games, I Haven't talked to this nigga since early yesterday and I know he see me calling and paging him."

I said so fast that I got a frog in my throat.

"where we going" she asked.

"I just need you to drop me off at his house" I said before ending the call.

I'm not even calling no more I said to myself.

When we pulled up in front of Audi house Tifa volunteered to wait for me, but I said she could leave after he opened the door.

I rung the doorbell a few times before he came and opened the door.

"What you tripping for" I yelled with anger and tears in my eyes.

"Man what you talking bout" he said as if nothing was wrong.

I walked into the house and he closed the door behind me. His parents were at work being it was Monday. I followed him upstairs to his bedroom and sat on the bed. "Audi what is going on with you? One minute your acting cool and the next your not" I said looking into his eyes trying to read his thoughts.
"Do you know how many times I called and paged you last night"
"Do you" I said
with the anger building back up.
"I know"
was all he said looking down at the floor.
"I don't have time for your bullshit"
I screamed and walked out of his room on my way out of his life.
"Fre wait" he said
chasing behind me.
He grabbed my arm just as I was unlocking the front door.
"I'm fucking mad" he screamed out as tears started rolling down his face.

I had never, I mean never seen Audi Tate
cry. He turned his body from me, but it was
too late I had saw the emotions that he tried
to keep hidden deep down inside.
"There getting a divorce" he said in a low
voice.
"That nigga been cheating on my mom" he
jumped up screaming.
I couldn't help, but cry with him.
I thought I knew Mr. and Mrs. Tate as much
as I knew there son, but I guess not. I
wondered to myself what could have caused
this. Mrs. Tate always seemed happy when I
was around, she had everything a wife could
ask for, a big lovely home, nice cars and her
loving family. Mr. Tate seemed like a nice
husband. He always took her out and he
always bought her nice gifts even when
there was no special occasion.
It was hard to believe. What could have
brought there relationship to this.
I couldn't imagine what Audi was feeling
partly because I didn't have my father

growing up for my mom too divorce.

"That bastard" he said before walking up the stairs to his room.

Why didn't he tell me sooner I thought to myself as I followed close behind.

I didn't say a word as we laid in silence.

I figured he would talk about it when he was ready.

"I'm not leaving" he said breaking the silence.

Any other time I would have been jumping for joy over those words, but it was a different situation and I knew he was talking out of anger.

He continued to talk and I listened.

I didn't respond,

how could I,

I didn't know what he was going through or did I,

Over the last month I felt as if I lost part of my family.

"Why would you take someone to dinner for their birthday, but give them bad news" he

said with more sadness than anger.
We sat through another long moment of
silence.
"I'm sorry" he said
in a whisper that was meant for only me to
hear.
"I'm sorry for acting like a asshole"
"I guess I get that from my pops" he said
with pain in his voice.
"Audi it's not your fault" was the first thing
that spilled out my mouth.
I didn't like hearing him talk like that.
I wished for his sake it was all a bad dream,
but it wasn't.
"We should have kept our baby"
"I should have never listened to him"
he went on to say as if it was nothing.
What did he mean by that, did Mr. Tate
know I was pregnant.
I thought to myself as I continued to lay
there.
We heard Mr. Tate come in the house and
was caught off guard when he opened the

door.

"Audi what you doing with this girl in here" He said standing in the door way.

"Not getting her pregnant" Audi replied just low enough for his dad not to hear him.

"We ain't doing nothing" unlike other people" Audi said loud enough for Mr. Tate to hear, as he was walking away from the doorway.

"What the hell you say boy" Mr. Tate yelled as he reappeared in the door way.

"I ain't say nothing" Audi said and started mumbling something else under his breath.

I had never heard Audi talk back to either of his parents.

He always treated them with respect, but I guess when you disrespect a boys mother no matter who you are they loose respect for you.

I wanted to call Tifa to pick me back up, but Audi wanted me to stay.

He thought if I was there it would keep him from hurting his father or his father hurting him.

We continued to lay around in the room watching BET.

Audi seemed a little better after getting everything off his chest, but at times he still cursed his dad and tried to hide his falling tears.

I climbed on top of him kissing him on his lips and working my way down to his neck.

I sucked on his neck until I could see a red strawberry mark appear.

I lifted his shirt and followed the familiar path down his chest with my tongue until I reached the rim of his basketball shorts.

CHAPTER 8

Tifa picked me up an hour before Mrs. Tate was due home. Audi preferred I stayed, but I didn't think his mom would have wanted to come home with a guest in the house.

I didn't want to see her in her time of pain either.

When I got in the car Tifa waited for me to say something, but I didn't know were to start.

I'm pretty sure she could tell I wasn't mad anymore.

"Don't repeat what I'm about to tell you" I said with a serious look on my face.

She knew if I said those words I meant it and I knew I could tell her without her telling anyone.

"Audi's parents are getting a divorce" I said and waited for her responds.

I could tell she didn't know how to respond just like I didn't. She knew it was bad, but just like me she never had to worry about that type of thing because her parents never married to divorce.

As bad as I wanted too I didn't tell her about the part that his dad wanted me to get the abortion.

I just knew that would set her off.

Tifa knew how much me and Audi loved each other she was our number one supporter when everybody else hated on our relationship.

"Girl I don't know what to say" she said shaking her head back and forth no.

"he cheated" I added with no hesitation.

It was hard to believe their relationship was on the line because they had been together for so long and seemed so happy together, but you really never know when your on the outside looking in.

Tifa rolled threw the projects where Lacy lived to see if she could see Deuces.

We parked in front of Lacy's building.

When we got out the car we could hear the music bumping from Lacy's window.

She always played her music loud for the whole neighborhood to hear.
As we walked towards her door we could see her leaning out the window.
"what's up y'all" she said
and made her way out the door to greet us.
"what's up girl"
I said shoving her, but not hard at all.
"what y'all about to do?"
She asked ready to join in our plans.
"I just picked up Fre from Audi's".
Tifa said looking in my direction.
"yeah we aint doing nothing just chillin"
I added.
"what's been up around here"
Tifa asked
There was always something happening in the projects
if it wasn't a fight, it was a killing,
if it wasn't a domestic violence, it was a child abuse.
They kept something going.
It had its good times too

with the house parties, water fights and crack heads making us laugh on a daily basis.

"nothing the po po's just ran through here chasing ROX. They say he stole a beer from the corner store" she replied

"did they catch him" me and tifa asked in unison.

"hell yeah they caught his slow fat ass" she said dancing to the music.

I felt faint so I sat in one of the plastic green chairs Lacy had on the porch. Lacy's auntie walked up holding a baby on her hip. The baby boy was bear footed and had on a dingy white t shirt with a saggy diaper. She put the baby down to retrieve a cigarette from her back pocket. The baby pounced up and down from the heat of the hot concrete.

"sorry lil man" she said as she pulled him up by the arm and placed him back on her hip.

"Lacy who the police was chasing" she asked with a grin on her face.

I felt my pager go off so I went into the

house to use the phone.

I picked up the cordless phone and dialed Audi's number. He picked up on the third ring. "whad up" he said

"hey what's up" I said back.

"where you at"

"I'm at Lacy's" I said and continued with asking how he was doing.

He said he was good, but that could mean anything just cause someone say there good doesn't really mean they are.

I asked about Mrs. Tate and he said she wasn't home yet.

"I'm just hanging out for a minute then I'm going home" I said and ended the conversation with I love you.

Lacy was still telling her auntie about Rox and the police when I got back outside.

She even demonstrated the way they tackled him to the ground.

The baby boy was sitting in the chair I had left and tried to get up when he saw me.

"It's ok lil man"

I said smiling at him. He was a cute lil boy if somebody just took the time to clean him up. My baby would never be that filthy I thought to myself.

"lets walk to the back" tifa said waiting for us to agree.

We walked towards the back of the projects in the direction of bomb's apartment. When we got to the back we sat on the meter box closest to the parking lot. There were some kids running around in the street and Hip was standing in the doorway of his apartment looking in our direction.

"hey Hip" we said together then busted out laughing.

We heard loud beating music when a candy red car on hundred spoke Dayton's pulled in the parking lot so fast I thought it would loose control and hit the meter box.

Deuces jumped out from the driver seat and bomb jumped out from the passenger seat. Both of them walked up to the apartment with black bags from the swap meet in there hands.

I don't know if they saw us or not the way they was moving to get in the house.

About a second later we saw the popo's roll by real slow looking in the parking lot.

That could explain deuces and bombs fast pace I thought to myself.

We sat out there talking with our other home girls as the sun started to set and the weather started to feel good. Deuces came out the door and stood on the porch. He looked over at the meter box and it wasn't long before he had our full attention. He didn't say a word before going backing the house.

"ooh look at deuces fine ass"

one of the home girls said aloud.

"That nigga too fine"

Another one said as she licked her lips and smacked them together.

I could tell tifa wanted to say something, but she knew it would be better not too.

Especially since she knew he was looking at only her.

The other home girls walked off towards the front of the projects and we knew Tifa wasn't leaving that spot until she talked to Deuces.

A lil while later Bomb came out the door and signaled for Tifa to come over. She told us to come with her so me and Lacy followed suit.

When we got over to the front door bomb told her to go in the house cause Deuces wanted her.

She was damn near in there before he could get the whole sentence out.

Bomb looked at me, but I looked away I wasn't about to get myself caught up in his eyes again.

"What's up Fre"
He said
"Nothing, what's up with you"
I said looking everywhere but at him.
"Why I didn't get a dance at the party"
He asked.
"cause you didn't ask for one"

I said sarcastically

"O so next time if I ask for one Ima get it?" He said with a smile.

"Maybe"

I said with a playful attitude.

"OK then we will see, I might just plan a party so I can get my dance with yo fine ass" he said and started laughing

Bomb invited me and Lacy inside, but it was getting late and I had to walk home. I didn't want to interrupt Tifa and I knew she was in good hands so Lacy walked me halfway home before we said our goodbyes and went our separate ways.

CHAPTER 9

Audi was leaving today and I had to see him before he left. Tifa was busy and his dad was at work so I had to catch the bus. He met me at the bus stop in front of the corner store. We went into the store to get some snacks and soda. On the way to his house we held hands and every chance we got we stopped and kissed. We made it to the house and went straight to Audi's room. I took off my shoes and got comfortable on the bed. Instead of turning on the TV. Audi turned on the radio and we laid in silence for awhile just listening to *R. Kelly's* CD. I broke the silence when I asked Audi if he really thought we could have a long distance relationship with him being in another state. He said we can try, but those weren't the words I was looking for I expected a hell yes.
The more I laid there under his arm I was starting to realize that this might be it for us.

He will be gone for over eight months before I saw him again. What will I be doing in that time or better yet what will he be doing.

Let mama tell it he will be meeting other people, seeing new things and laying out the path for the rest of his life.

That's what she claim happens when you go away to college and that's what she wanted for me so maybe I should want the same for Audi even if it doesn't include me.

Audi could tell I was frantic about the whole situation and tried to reassure me that our long distance relationship would work.

"I will call you everyday" he promised

"I will be waiting by the phone" I said teary eyed

"Did you start your college applications" he asked

"Yes I did a few"

I said with no enthusiasm

because I had never really thought about college. I didn't know one single person in college or who went to college so it wasn't something I thought about. I was just trying to graduate from high school.

"Did you apply for Arizona" he asked

"YES"

I said with an attitude that he quickly dismissed.

He knew I was upset about the whole thing so he tried to make me feel better.

He started singing in my ear then he climbed on top of me. He kissed me around my neck and pulled off my shirt, then my shorts. He then unhooked my bra and slid off my panties.

He got out of the bed and locked the door. He went over to the nightstand and opened the drawer in search of a condom.

He lifted the same envelope that was once in the center console of the car and found the box of Trojan condom he was looking for. He quickly undressed his self and rolled the condom over his hard penis.

He climbed back on top of me, but before

entering my private property he asked if I was alright.
I gave him the ok to complete his mission.
As I happily accepted the pleasure I was receiving I thought to myself
could this be the last time
I made love to my love Audi Tate.
Before leaving I helped Audi pack the rest of his stuff including our framed photo that he kept on his dresser and I made sure he knew that's where he should put it when he got to his dorm room.
"I need to get some more boxes out the garage"
he said and left the room.
As I was putting his hygiene in the empty box I thought about the envelope that kept popping up in my mind and walked over to the night stand drawer.
I opened the drawer and pulled out the baby blue envelope I could feel the card still inside. I pulled out the card
To a very special person

It read on the cover with hearts decorated all around it. I opened the inside of the card and a picture fell out. Before I could pick up the 4x6 photo my eyes zoomed right into the words written in the card

Love Your sweetheart,
Samantha Tate

My body filled with anger as I reached to the floor to pick up the falling photo. It was ugly ass Samantha with her four eyed ass.

"Hell naw" I screamed

Just as Audi was walking into the room

"Fre what happened"

He said not knowing what I had just discovered

I turned around to face him.

The picture in one hand, the card in the other and pain in between.

I was so mad I couldn't speak and tears started rolling down my cheeks. Audi starred at me as I starred at him. The seconds of silence seemed liked hours.

I quickly snapped out of the short daze my

mind had went into and started demanding answers.

"why the hell do you have a birthday card from this bitch" I said

And before he could answer I was on to the next question.

"and why the hell is she calling herself Samantha Tate"

"please don't tell me you fucking around with that bitch again" I screamed

Him standing there speechless with his head down gave me all the confirmation I needed.

"your no better than your dad" I said as I walked pass him pushing the card and picture into his chest and walked out the room and possibly out of his life.

I left out the front door slamming it behind me and ran all the way to the bus stop.

I had just made it when the bus was pulling up. I took a seat in the back right behind the rear door. I could see Audi standing at the corner waving the bus down as it passed.

I laid my head against the window and

closed my eyes trying to hold back the tears that were slowly building up. A stream of tears managed to escape out the crest of my right eye and rolled down my neck.

In seconds I replaced the tears with anger and by the time I got home the anger was back to tears.

Mama just so happen to be in the living room when I walked through the front door. I was hoping I could go straight to my room without conversation, but that didn't happen.

"hey mama" I said in a low voice that barely reached her.

"hey Fre where you coming from" she asked not taking her eyes off the television.

"I just left Audi's house you know he leaving today" I said as I quickly thought to myself that could be the excuse for my teary eyes and sad face if she was to ask.

But she didn't she just continued with her show and left me to be.

I went into my room and shut the door. I laid across my bed and cried as hard as my heart would allow me to.

The constant vibration from my pager mixed with the vibration of my aching chest and I didn't bother to notice it.

I slept for two hours before waking to the ring of the telephone.

"hello" I said into the receiver for a second forgetting what all had happened in the hours leading up to this moment until I heard his voice on the other end calling my name.

"Fre, Fre, Freira" he called out in desperation.

"don't call me call that bitch" I replied "and don't call my house no more" I said right before slamming the phone down and hanging up.

He called over and over again. I turned the ringer off to stop the ringing.

A few times throughout that night he called mama's line, but I told Mani not to answer and Mama did come in once to tell me, but I lied and told her I was busy and would call him back.

CHAPTER 10

It had been almost two weeks since Audi left for college.

I was getting use to not having him around. I spent more time with the girls and hanging out in the projects. He called me everyday as promised, but I didn't answer for the first three days. When I did finally start taking his calls He begged for me to forgive him and take him back, I forgave him, but I didn't want him back. Once a cheater always a cheater I would say to him every time he tried convincing me to give him another chance.

I had dedicated to many years of my life to our relationship and all he did was lead me on making me think we were going to be together forever, getting me pregnant making me have an abortion and to top it off cheating on me. Hell naw I didn't want him back.

Lacy had called earlier that day to ask what

time I was coming over. It wasn't a matter of if I was coming since that's were I had spent most of my time since Audi had left.

After doing some chores around the house I got dressed and called Tifa to pick me up. She wasn't home so I called Lacy to see if she was at her house.

Lacy picked up on the first ring as if she was waiting on my call.

"hey girl you ready" she said before greeting me with a hello.

"yeah is Tifa over there" I said hearing her voice in the background

"yeah we about to come get you" Lacy said and hung up the phone.

In a hurry I untied the bandana from around my ponytail and used the end of the damped towel to wipe away the brown gel that had dried around my hairline.

I ran into the bathroom and quickly lined my lips with the black eyeliner pencil then glossing them with Vaseline. Before I could make it back to my room there was a knock on the door.

I opened the door to let Tifa and Lacy in and they followed me back into my room.

"I'm ready y'all" I said as I gathered the things off my bed and threw them in my purse.

On the way out the room I picked up the bottle of Victoria Secret body spray and sprayed myself down with the flowery sent.

I locked up the house and got into the white Hyundai that awaited.

When we got to Lacy's apartment we didn't bother going inside, instead we walked to the back of the projects where we had been constantly hanging out.

Hip noticed us right away and started his usual playing.

"there they go" he yelled out in our direction "don't beat me up y'all" he screamed out as we got closer to him

He always said stuff to make us laugh.

"what's happening back here" Lacy asked Hip

"shit you know same thang" he replied.
Bomb, Dueces and DJ was standing out on the porch when we walked up.
Tifa walked over and stood by Dueces who she was now seeing on a regular basis.
Bomb and I had also had conversation the last few days.
Nothing major just hi and bye with a little flirting in between.
He often kept reminding me about the slow dance I still owed to him and I promised him he would get it.
We all sat in front of the apartment for awhile talking and listening to the music that was coming from Hip's apartment which was next door.
A car pulled up and Hip jumped from his chair and ran out to the driver's window.
He returned to his chair a minute later with a fist of balled up money.
Over the past week I had noticed this was one of his usual routines.
I watched as he straightened out the

crumbled five dollar bill and four single dollar bills before stuffing them into his pocket.

Whatever he was selling, they were sure buying I thought to myself

"The next one on me"

DJ said

aloud to no one in particular.

It was around 4pm and hot as hell outside. Deuces went inside and Tifa followed behind him.

"shid I'm bout to go in here too and get some of this AC" Bomb said

looking at me and Lacy as an invitation for us to come in.

We both raised from the chairs and followed behind him into the apartment.

Deuces and Tifa had already made their way into one of the bedrooms.

Me and Lacy both sat on the couch and took in the nice cool air that blew from the vent above our heads.

"y'all want a soda" Bomb asked

walking towards us with two already in his hands.

He sat them down on the glass coffee table that sat in front of the couch.

He took a seat in the recliner that was next to the end of the couch closes to where I was sitting.

Before he got too comfortable there was a knock at the door.

He looked through the peep hole before opening it.

Hip walked in with a brown paper bag in one hand and more balled up money in the other. He walked into the kitchen setting the paper bag on the kitchen table and this time straightening out what seemed to be more than the nine dollars he had collected earlier. I picked up the soda from the glass table and popped it open. Taking a sip and glancing around the apartment in between more sips. It was my first time back in the apartment since the party and it looked pretty decent with all the furniture back in its regular

place. Unlike Lacy's apartment it was only one level and much cleaner. You could tell a woman lived there by the décor. There were tall standing plants in each corner of the living room and a black naked couple statue that sat in the center of the coffee table with matching lamps that sat on each end table.
"y'all cool" Bomb asked
on his way back into the living room and sitting in the chair that he had not too long ago left.
"yeah I'm cool I said and looked at Lacy.
"yeah I'm alright" she said
Bobbing her head to the low music that Bomb had coming from the floor speakers. Hip turned the paper bag over dumping small clear baggies out on the kitchen table. They all were filled with lime green marijuana. He opened one of the baggies and dumped the continence on the table top.
"tell Deuces to come on so we can hit this shit" hip said
looking in Bombs direction.

Bomb got up from the recliner and walked towards the back.

"y'all smoking"

Hip asked me and Lacy with a curious look on his face.

Me and Lacy looked at each other

"yeah" we both said in unison and smiled. We weren't considered smokers, but we had smoked a few times before.

Our first time was at my cousin house, she had asked me to come over and baby sit while she went out to party. Tifa and Lacy went with me.

We found a half smoked joint in her ash tray and smoked it. We thought she would be too hung over the next day to notice it was gone, but of course when it comes to weed she remembered. She didn't get mad though, she just had her cousin to cousin talk with us about smoking weed.

Don't be smoking with no any and everybody

She said

and if you don't see them roll it, don't hit it.
After the lecture she rolled a fat joint and we got high.

Bomb came back in the living room with Tifa and Deuces following right behind him. Tifa came and sat in between me and Lacy on the couch. Deuces and Hip pulled chairs from the kitchen into the living room and Bomb got comfortable back in the recliner. Hip pulled a lighter from his pants pocket and held the fire to the end of the philly that hung from his lips. He blew a big cloud of grey smoke into the air and sucked most of the smoke back into his mouth. After taking another hit he passed it to Bomb who was sitting on his left. Bomb repeated the act then passed it to me. I held the blunt up to my lips and took a big hit, inhaling some of the smoke and blowing out the rest I began to choke. I passed the blunt to Tifa who copied my actions then passed it to Lacy who took more than the one puff that me and Tifa was able to take. The boys joked about how Lacy was handling the weed. She passed it on to Deuces who took his few hits then we repeated the rotation.

Deuces got up and opened the patio door to let some of the smoke escape out.

We ended up smoking another blunt before Hip left and Lacy ended up leaving too. Deuces and Tifa went back into the bedroom and Bomb came and sat next to me on the couch. We started talking and getting to know each other more on a personal level. He asked about my boyfriend and for the first time in a long time I could say I didn't have one, but I didn't, I avoided that subject by saying next subject.

As the time passed we laughed and flirted with each other. I felt real comfortable around him.

It was a little after 9 p.m. when we left their house and already had made plans to come back the next day.

I called mama to let her know I was staying the night at Tifa's and would be home first thing in the morning. Me and Tifa stayed up most of the night talking about Bomb and Deuces. I had to admit to her that I was really starting to feel Bomb.

"I cant wait to see my boo tomorrow" I said with excitement that went straight through my body.

"oh yo boo huh" Tifa said laughing

She hadn't seen me act that way over anybody, but Audi.

"yes my boo" I said laughing with her. The rest of the night we took turns exchanging stories about what happened that day. I found out that Tifa gave it up to Deuces and was now deep in love and I would soon learn I wasn't too far behind her.

CHAPTER 11

Mama saw the happiness that I couldn't hide written all over my face and quickly questioned what it was about. I didn't tell her about Bomb because she would have started with her same old stuff.
Tifa was coming back to get me in an hour so I got dress in a hurry putting on my favorite booty shorts and white tank top
My phone rung four times before I picked up without reading the caller I.D.
"Hello" I said
"Damn you never home" Audi said waiting for my responds
"Ok"
"what's up"
I said irritated by his greeting
"what you doing"
"you busy" he asked
"Yeah,
getting ready to go" I responded
"where you going" he asked

"umm why" I replied
"ok it's like that" he said angry
"I'm going somewhere with Tifa"
"and your not my man so I really don't have to explain that to you"
I quickly replied and hung up.
Audi had been calling my house and blowing up my pager everyday since he left. I had to keep reminding him we weren't together and I was happy being single. He didn't seem to understand so I had to be mean at times just to get the point across. Tifa was back within an hour and I was ready as promised. By the time we made it to the projects Audi had paged me hella times. I knew he would keep paging until I called him so I turned it off and threw it in my purse. Bomb, Deuces and Hip were gathered around the meter box along with some other dudes having a debate about who would win a slap boxing contest between Bomb and one of the dudes. It quickly heated up when bomb caught the slim dude

off guard with a slap to the head. The slim dude showed his quick reflexes when he slapped Bomb back, hitting him across the chin. They both took ground away from the meter box on a dry patch of grass and began walking around in a circle with there hands up and palms open. They both took turns slapping at each other until they got tired. I laughed at the childishness they both showed when trying to determine a winner. After getting the votes of us bystanders it was declared a tie. Me and Tifa sat close by on the hood of her car and held our on conversation while watching the boys who had started a crap game on the concrete. Bomb called me over to blow on the dice, he said it was for luck. I must had really been lucky to him because after each roll he picked up the dollar bills that laid in the center of the circle. After watching them play for awhile I caught on to the game and Bomb put up a dollar for me to play against one of the dudes. He ended up taking my dollar because I rolled snake eyes on my first roll.

Tifa even tried and won three dollars before feeling too lucky and putting it all up on one roll.

"DAM" everyone witness to the crap out yelled in unison

The slim dude ended up with the majority of the winnings before we all called it quits.

The dudes hung around for awhile longer before finally leaving in a beat up two door hoompty.

Me and Tifa was in the middle of a conversation when Bomb came up behind me and put his arms through mine locking his hands with my hands.

"don't we look good together"

he said to Tifa who was standing in front of us.

"Tifa this my girl" he said

still holding on to me like we were posing for a prom picture.

Tifa only responded with a laugh.

That was the closes we had ever been to each other and the heat from both our bodies send a cold chill down my back. I didn't respond, but gave Tifa a surprising look as thought ran wild in my head.

Did I really just let him claim me and not dispute it?

Was I really ready for another relationship so soon?

What would Audi say if he knew I was now taken?

The cold chill was gone and I broke out into a sweat.

Maybe I'm over reacting I thought to myself as I felt my body calming down.

"I'm hot, you wanna go to the store and get a soda" Tifa asked

Freeing me from my thoughts.

Tifa placed the orange Shasta soda and bag of Funyuns on the counter top and picked through the jug of now n laters until she found four green ones.

After paying for her snacks she moved to the

side so I could pay for my soda. Before I could place the strawberry Shasta on the counter top Bomb had taken it out my hand and added it to his arm full of goodies. "Let me get a philly swisher" he said to the cashier as he plopped all the items on the counter top. He pulled out a neatly folded stack of bills. He flipped through the stack of twenties until he came to a ten dollar bill and pulled it fast from in between the other bills not messing up the stack. "This all you wanted" he asked as he handed me the strawberry Shasta. "Yes, thank you" I said with a smile.

On the way back to the projects Tifa walked ahead while me and Bomb walked side by side exchanging small talk. He asked simple questions like how old was I, what grade was I in and did I have any sisters or brothers, but nothing again about if I had a boyfriend.

"Why they call you Bomb" I asked before I knew it.

"Because I got that bomb baby" he responded with a sexy laugh that I had never heard come from him before. I don't know what turned me on more the responds to the question or the laugh.

"O" I said and laughed with him.

"Well what is your real name Bommmb" I asked

"What's your real name Freeee" he said grabbing my hand and locking it with his before we crossed the street and walked through the center of the projects towards his house. We went back and forth on who should tell there real name first then he gave in when he figured out I wasn't giving up.

"Samuel" he said

then a brief silence followed before I told him he didn't look like a Samuel and asked if he was named after his dad. I assumed his dad was never in the picture the way he bad mouthed him and cursed after the question. Come to find out he was dead on top of all that. I felt sorry after I asked, but I kinda knew how he felt with my dad not being there and all.

"My real name is Freira and they call me Fre with one E for short"

I said trying to lighten the subject, but I could tell talking about his dad hit a nerve and it seemed like he still had it on his mind. When we made it to the house Deuces was pulling out the parking lot with Tifa sitting in the passenger seat. Tifa waved bye and Deuces threw up his gang sign, burning rubber and blasted his rap music down the street. We stood at the corner until the car disappeared.

"Dang it's hot in here" Bomb said when we walked in the house.

"Aint you hot" he asked waiting for me to agree. I knew how people was about blowing there air conditioner in the middle of the day so I said I was alright plus his mom had a few fans blowing throughout the house.

He unplugged one of the fans and headed

towards his room calling me to follow behind him. I sat on the messy unmade bed not knowing I had sat on the TV remote until he started looking for it. After realizing I had sat on it I joked with him about making his bed next time. He flipped back and forth from BET to MTV trying to catch some new music video that was recently released. When the video finally came on he boogied and rapped along with the song. It was funny, but sexy the way he grooved to the music. He danced his way across the room to his tall oak wood dresser. He opened the top drawer and dung underneath all the clothes that filled it. He pulled out a sandwich bag that was half way filled with marijuana that stunk up the room as soon as he opened it. He stuck his fingers in the bag pulling out just enough to fill the philly blunt that hung out his shirt pocket. He unwrapped the philly from the plastic and licked it up and down a few times before using his thumb nail to split it down the middle. He dumped the tobacco from the philly on top of the dresser and picked up pinches of the marijuana spreading it throughout the philly. After getting all the marijuana to fit inside the philly I watched him like a hawk as he began to use his tongue and lips to close the philly back up. *I could sit and watch him roll blunts all day.* I thought to myself.

After watching those sexy ass lips tongue kiss that blunt it was my turn.

I didn't know how it would happen, but I knew I wanted a taste.

He didn't take his eyes off me, holding the lit lighter in one hand and running the sides of the blunt up and down the fire with the other hand, it was like he was trying to hypnotize me and I wasn't going to stop him.

"Damn" he said after noticing he almost burnt a hole in the blunt.

"Girl you gone make me burn up the weed" he said,

holding the fire to one end of the blunt until it was lit with a bright red tip. He puffed, puffed and puffed again before passing it to me. I puffed it one good time and passed it back. We continued the rotation until it was gone.

We both were laid back on his bed, the fan was blowing, we were high and I was feeling good. For a while we laid in silence and only our bodies did the talking and they communicated well. He climbed on top of me and started his hypnosis again, but this time I was going all the way under.

Before I knew it our tongues were tied and lips were locked. He rubbed my body as we continued to kiss. After pulling his lips from mine he slowly began to pull my shirt and bra off at the same time. I looked up at him with my arms still above my head and nipples sitting up hard as uncooked beans. He went back and forth using his tongue to play with each nipple before stuffing one whole titi in his mouth. We finally got down to business and business was good. Deuces and Bomb dropped me and Tifa off up the street from my house. I didn't want Deuces pulling up that late at night with his music blasting for mama to come out wanting to know who they were. I called it right cause when we got in the house mama was still up in the living room watching TV. Me and Tifa went straight to my room and closed the door. We instantly began talking about what we had been doing since we last saw each other earlier that day. As she started going on and on about what her and Deuces did I was contemplating on wether or not to tell her ALL me and Bomb did. As I continued to listen to Tifa I couldn't help getting caught up in my own thoughts. The thought of being in a new relationship brought butterflies to my stomach, happy butterflies the kind that have you feeling like your floating in air. I was happy, happy, but scared all at the same time.

CHAPTER 12

One year later……………….

It was the last day of school and graduation was a week away. It just so happened Lacy's Birthday fell on graduation weekend and even though ½ credit kept her from walking she still had a reason to celebrate.

We had already started planning for a big graduation/birthday bash.

Lacy's mom didn't have a problem when Lacy told her we were having it at her house. She was cool like that.

Bomb and I were fine. For the past year we spent just about everyday together. On the days Tifa had to stay after school I would catch the school bus with Lacy to the projects. A lot of times Bomb used Deuces car to pick me up from school and every time I would have an audience of school kids staring at the suped up car as I climbed in. He would always have the newest cash money CD blasting through the 12inch speakers. If Lacy knew he was picking me up she would still catch the school bus home. Even though Bomb didn't mind she would feel like she was intruding.

After school I always hung out with Bomb until 8 o'clock which was my curfew, even though I was now eighteen mama said I was under curfew until I graduated, but knowing her she would still have some kinda say so on what I was doing.

She already been saying I'm not a kid anymore and if I wasn't going to college I needed to be looking for a job so I can help with bills. Little do she know I wanted a job so I could move out.

Even though mama made enough money to take care of us she always said grown people should be able to take care of they self and that's what I was going to do.

Mama had met Bomb for the first time on my birthday. He tried to surprise me with a bear and balloons, but mama opened the door and got my surprise before I could. As she went out looking for the person who rung the bell and disappeared she was met by a 5'4" boy wearing jean shorts that were so low off his butt they could have passed for pants.

Bomb was just surprised as she was as he stuttered for words. "I, I, I'm sorry mam, umm is Fre here"

I could hear him say as I walked out the front door and found him and my mom standing in front of the bush he had once been hiding behind.

"BOMB" I said, more surprised as I would have been if I had opened the door to find the bear and balloons myself.

Mama turned around and handed me the big brown bear attached to the floating balloons that had happy birthday written in different ways all around them.

Mama went back in the house and me and Bomb sat on the porch.

I couldn't stop laughing at the way he reacted to mama, I had never saw him like that, but he had good reasons to be intimidated, she was good at intimidating people. After he calmed his nerves I told him he would have to go inside and formally introduce his self or mama would have a big problem. If nothing else she demanded respect and if you come in, around or near her house you better speak.
"Dammm baby,
I thought she was at work"
he said rubbing his head, still embarrassed.
"naw today is my birthday" I said trying to hold in the laughter.
"how did you get here" I said looking up and down the street for Deuces ride.
I knew it had to be close by because Bomb wasn't the type to just get dropped off anywhere especially now that he and his homies had been into it with a rival gang that had jumped one of his lil homies and in return they badly beaten one of their homies

putting him in the hospital.

"I got dropped off, trying to surprise yo butt" he said breaking his seriousness down to a laugh.

"no you didn't" I said as I kept scoping the neighborhood for Mary, Mary was the name Deuces gave his car. When I first heard the name I thought he was crazy along with the fact that he would even take time to name his car.

"you ready to go in and introduce yourself to my mom" I asked after realizing this fool did get dropped off.

When we walked in mama was in the kitchen washing dishes.

"Mama this is Sam" I said shoving my elbow in his side letting him know to say something.

"hello Miss" he said rubbing his head nervously.

"next time I find a gift at my door I'm keeping it" she said lightning the subject with a laugh.

"ok" he said "next time ima make sure I bring two" he added.

Feeling good that she didn't go too hard on him.

We stayed and talked with mama until she figured out who all she knew in his family. Come to find out she went to school with two of his aunties and dated one of his older cousins back in the day.

Mama was one of the few people you meet that was actually born and raised in Las Vegas and growing up on the Westside she knew a lot of people and their family.

After listening to mama short stories about Bomb's older cousin me and Bomb went back outside.

"what y'all gonna do fo yo birthday" he asked

"just going out to eat" I responded

"well let me take this boy back his car before he start looking for me" he laughed.

"where's Mary, I thought you said you got dropped off" I said punching him in the gut.

"Damn babe" he said folding over.

I watched as he jogged to the corner where he had left Mary.

Although he was out of sight I could hear the exhaust pipes when he started her up followed by the music blasting through the speakers.

I stood outside until the distinctive sound was gone.

At dinner mama still talked about Bomb's family, but mostly his older cousin. She must have really had a thing for him.

"Yeah Freira they aint no joke, they like us" meaning her and her brothers.

"they'll split yo head" she said with hype in her voice.

Mama and her brothers where well known around Vegas. They made a lot of trouble in their younger days. If you looked at mama now you wouldn't believe the things she say she did when she was younger, I wouldn't believe it if it wasn't for other people telling me how much of a terror she was and having

all brothers didn't make it no better.
I cringe inside every time she tells me the story of how my sperm donor put his hands on her and she sliced three of his fingers almost decapitating them. Then my uncles all went over there and beat him to a bloody pope.
I told that nigga I would cut him up like a Christmas turkey, she said she told him.
I cracked up laughing every time I heard that part of the story.
After the bell rang me, Tifa and Lacy gathered in the front of the school signing yearbooks, taking pictures and saying our last goodbyes to some.
Bomb finally made it through the line of cars waiting for their passengers.
Just as we were pulling off, a fight broke out.
Just in time. I thought to myself.
I didn't need to be involved with anything that could keep me from walking across that stage. *Hopefully Tifa and Lacy don't stick*

around too long either. We were known for keeping up mess as the dean would say. It wasn't that, we just kept people in their place and if someone had a problem we made sure it got solved.

From the rearview mirror I could see people running from the parking lot towards the crowd of people that had created a ring around the fight and the further we drove the larger the crowd got. I had a good laugh inside wondering who had been fighting.

CHAPTER 13

Mama pulled the long silky straight hair over my shoulders and sat the navy blue cap on my head holding it in place with one hand as she forced open the hair pin with her teeth. After securing the cap to my head she stood back and smiled.

"please don't start crying again cause you gonna make me cry and mess up my makeup" I said hoping the tears that were already build up in the pit of her eyes would just disappear. I knew mama was happy, this was all she had talked about the last few weeks.

Mama dropped me off in front of the Thomas and Mack Center and left in search of a parking space. I followed the arrow on the sign pointing towards the graduates entrance. Tifa, Lacy and some of the home girls were standing outside the lines waiting for me.

I handed Lacy a ticket to get into the graduation. I could feel the pounding in her chest and hear the weep of her tears when I gave her a big hug.

I felt bad because I knew she had did everything she could to walk with us and all just wasn't enough.

"Y'all hurry up, it's almost time to get lined up" Tifa said

Leading us into the moving line of graduates entering the building.

My heart was racing as I entered the big arena packed with people. I tried not looking into the crowd as I took the long walk to my seat.

I was Blinded by camera flashes every time I tried to look for mama in the area she was seated. I finally spotted her out when I heard Bomb, my uncles and cousin yell out Fre during a pause in the speech. I was surprise to see how many of my family members showed up including my grandpa. Seeing him always brought instant memories of my granny and I wish she could have been here to see this.

My row was finally called to line up for our diplomas. The laughter, screams and tears of happiness from the crowd sent excitement through my bones.

"Angelica Burk,"

"Thomas Burne,"

"Freira D Burns." The announcer said as Mr. Harp, *the principal* handed me my diploma and shook my hand. I walked carefully across the stage hoping not to trip in the six inch heels as I posed for pictures. It took about thirty minutes before they finally got to the *L's* and I couldn't wait to see my best friend walk the stage as I had just did.

"Latifa Lee" the announcer said as Tifa got her diploma from Mr. Harp and walked across the stage posing for pictures too.

At the end of the ceremony all the graduates stood for the turning of the tassels. This was the most memorable part of the ceremony because this was the end and the beginning of a new chapter of our lives.

Cameras flashed as tassels turned and caps were thrown high in the air. We had did it! It was a large crowd at the end of the tunnel we exited from. Bomb found me as I searched the crowd looking for him and my family. He had a bouquet of colorful flowers that he handed me with a big hug and kiss to top it off. He lead me to the direction of where mama and them were. I ran to mama and embraced her with hugs and kisses along with my other family.

We all went back to the house were mama had cooked up a big celebration dinner and invited the whole family. Mrs. Lee even came with her famous banana pudding.

As I looked around the house full of people I saw joy and laughter. Folks playing cards, some line dancing to the music and kids running through the house with balloons that were once taped to the wall. As I watched my mother sitting at the card table I could see the joy that covered her face, she was proud, proud of me and what I had a achieved that day.

Once the party died down and everyone went about their way I helped mama clean up.

"Freira honey I'm so proud of you" mama cried while holding me in her arms.

That's all she wanted, for me to walk across that stage and receive my diploma mainly because I wouldn't be able to get a good job without it and because her or her brothers never got theirs.

The phone rang, interrupting mama's emotional moment.

I picked up without screening the caller ID.

"Hello" I said into the receiver

"Hey Fre is this you" Audi said

"Yes is me, what's up maaan" I said playfully

I could tell he was surprise by my playfulness because when he spoke next it sounded more uplifting than when he first asked for me.

I hadn't talked to him in a while. He had stop calling so much after finally finding out I was in a relationship with Bomb. When he first found out he called cussing me out, blowing up my pager with 187, 304 and whatever other hidden message through numbers he could think of sending. He finally got over it and after apologizing, crying and threatening to beat up somebody if I didn't accept his sorries I gave in and agreed to still be friends.

"Congrads on making it across that stage" he said

"Thank you" I replied with joy

It meant something to me that he would remember my graduation and call to congratulate me. We had been through so many up's and down's and it seemed like we were still going through it even though we weren't together.

I didn't think I loved him anymore, but I knew I still cared about him and his feelings.

"Are you going out" he asked

"Well mama cooked and we had a little get together here. Everybody just left a little while ago" I said

"So you not gonna do nothing tonight" he asked

"No I'm staying in plus me and the girls having a birthday/graduation bash this weekend.

"Who birthday" he asked

"Lacy's" I said

"O that's cool, be careful" he said. Anytime I told him I was hanging out or going to a party he would tell me to be careful. Even when we were together he was always protective about me hanging out. I could understand that with all the shit that happens.

"I will" I said

"I love you Freira" he said

"I love you too" I said before ending the call.

I didn't want to tell Audi I was really getting

ready to go to the movies with Bomb, Tifa and Deuces. He would have had a million and one questions.

Tifa picked me up. We met Bomb and Deuces at there house. Bomb rode with me in Tifa's car and Tifa rode with Deuces. Tifa and Deuces relationship was different. After falling head over hills for him she soon found out he was a player. He didn't have just one girl and if you wanted to be one of his girls you knew you had to take it as it came. That didn't mean they all accepted it that way. I'd seen him go off on one female so bad after she popped up over their house without calling or being asked to come. Tifa found out the hard way. She had been blowing up his pager, but he wouldn't return her call so she popped up over there knowing I was there at the time. I knew he was in his bedroom with a female, but didn't want to hurt her feelings so I said I hadn't seen him. She banged on his bedroom door and sure enough he opened it and cursed her out before slamming it in her face.

The next day he called her to come over as if nothing happened. I couldn't believe that she would still fuck with him, but she did. She said it's the way he made her feel, Like a woman.

I didn't quite understand that, but if she liked it I had to love it.

I followed Mary through the parking lot as Deuces swerved her through standing cars in front of the theatre. We were on our second lap through the parking lot before he finally pulled into a parking space closes to the back and I parked the white Hyundai two spaces down from him.

Bomb and I got out and walked over to Deuces car. We hopped in the back seat and Deuces put a fat blunt into rotation. Since being with them, me and Tifa had became regular weed smokers.

It was 9:15 and the movie was starting in five minutes so we hurried out the car and made our way into the theatre.

After the movie me and Bomb hung out in the parking lot while Deuces and Tifa went about there way. Tifa didn't mind me keeping her car when she was with Deuces as long as I kept gas in it and kept it clean. She'd rather be in Mary any chance she got. I sat on the trunk of the car while Bomb talked it up with DJ, West and a few more of his home boys who were out there. As I was grooving to the music I had playing from the stereo I couldn't help but listen to the boys heated conversation about the nigga's they had been getting into it with.

"Them nigga's don't want none" West kept repeating to his self as he shook his head.

"Man let me catch one of them nigga's slippin and I'ma show um" DJ added with his hand on his waistband.

Soon as we drove out the parking lot Bomb pulled his cellular phone from his pocket and dialed Deuces.

"Bro's them bitch nigga's trippin hard" he yelled into the receiver

"them nigga's been rolling by lil Whoopie mama house all day just lookin she said"
"Naw DJ, West and them was out there after the movie telling me that shit"
"ok I'll see you back at the crib man" he finished then hung up the phone and placing it back in his pocket.

I didn't quite know what had started all this mess, but I had a feeling it wasn't going to end so good. They had been back and forth since last year when Bomb lil homie got jumped and they went back and retaliated. Last I heard he was out of the hospital, but they left him crippled.

When we got back to the projects Deuces and Tifa was sitting out on the meter box. Bomb followed Deuces into the house were I suppose they were going to talk about what was going on.

"Do you know what's going on" Tifa asked concerned

"I don't know" I said not wanting to give up wrong information since I really didn't know myself.

"what did Deuces say" I asked

"He didn't say nothing, I just could tell he was upset about something after talking with Bomb" she said

Deuces came out and Bomb signaled for me to come inside. He told me he had to go take care of some business and he would call me when he got back home. Deuces must had told Tifa the same because when I walked outside she was already in the car waiting for me to come out.

Tifa dropped me off at home and promised to call me when she made it home.

CHAPTER 14

The next morning I woke up feeling new. I had nobody school to go to and nobody to answer to. I was grown and about to do my own thang.

I opened the blinds to let the sun light shine through and begun cleaning up my room. Once I started, it turned into deep cleaning. I changed my room around and cleaned out my closet. I didn't realize all the stuff from Me and Audi's relationship I was still holding on too. I got rid of it all plus some other things from my younger past life. Today was the beginning of my new adult life.

I laid back on the neatly made bed and blew out a sign of relief, I was finish cleaning. Breaking News ran across the television screen as the reporter started to speak. I quickly turned down the stereo and listened in on the reporter.

Shots fired in a valley neighborhood late last

night hitting two people, A man in his late fifties and a teen. The man is in critical condition here at UMC and the teen has died from his gunshot wounds. Metro detectives says it appears to be gang related.
I picked up the phone on the first ring, with my eyes still glued to the TV.

It was Lacy calling to tell me about the shooting last night and who it was that was killed.

Lacy was always the one to get the street gossip first. Manly because she had kinfolk in just about every neighborhood in Las Vegas.

"Girl Baby boy got killed last night" she said

"what, that's crazy, what happened"

"they said it was a drive by" she said

She also brought up the fact that Lil Whoopie and them had been beefing with Baby boy and his crew and she felt they might have had something to do with it. I didn't entertain her concerns although I had thought about if the business Bomb and Deuces had to handle the night before had anything to do with it.

"You ready for the party tomorrow" I said changing the subject

"Yeah I'm waiting for auntie to bring the food stamps so I can get the chicken wings and soda" she said

Lacy was excited about the party and so was I, but I had to admit I had other things on my mind.

After finding out that bit of information from Lacy I called Tifa.

She picked up on the first ring. Before I could speak she asked if I heard about Baby boy getting killed. I asked her how she find out and she said she saw it on the news, but didn't know who it was until Lacy called and told her. Our conversation soon changed from the shooting to the party we were having the next day.

We talked about what we intended on wearing and who all we thought would show up. Being it was at Lacy house we knew it would be a big turn out, like I said Lacy had kinfolk all over Vegas and they always seemed to know about any party that was happening at her house.

I asked if she had spoken to Deuces and she hadn't. She asked me the same question and I had the same answer. She picked me up and we rode to the projects. I knocked on the door while she sat in the car and waited. Lois opened the door. She said the boys weren't there she hadn't seen them since earlier. Tifa and I walked through the projects to Lacy's house. Lacy was gone to the store to get the chicken and soda for the party so we walked back to the car. Just as we were about to pull off Deuces and Bomb were pulling into the parking lot.

We followed them into the house. I went with Bomb in his room ad Tifa with Deuces. The evening news happened to be on and they were again talking about the shooting. They didn't have anybody in custody for the shooting, but had a description of the car used in the drive by.

Bomb study the TV closely as the reporter gave details about the shooting. "that's crazy huh" I said trying to end the uncomfortable silence

"hell yeah nigga's be slippin" he responded, eyes still on the TV.

He went to the top drawer and pulled out the zip lock bag of weed. Deuces came knocking on the door. Bomb stood outside the door exchanging a few quick words with Deuces before coming back in. As he rolled the blunt he reminded me about the movie we went to see last night and if anybody was to ask. He, Deuces, Tifa and I came back to the house and stayed in for the rest of the night. I already knew why he was telling me that as a matter of fact he had just confirmed my curiosity about what type of business he went to handle.

After leaving Tifa told me about the similar conversation she had with Deuces. The drive home was quieter than usual and we both seemed to be in deep thought.

What a way to start off adult hood, I thought to myself.

I checked my caller ID and saw that Bomb had called me three times. Two times earlier and once since I had left his house. Since he'd gotten that cellular phone he called and paged me way more than before. I dialed his cell number and he picked up on the first ring. He said he was just calling to check on me and asked what time I would be in the neighborhood getting ready for the party tomorrow.

I told him the party didn't start until eight and me and the girls were meeting up by 4 o'clock to decorate, then me and Tifa was going to her house to get dress.

He thought I should get ready for the party at his house then he and I could walk to the party together.

So I agreed.

CHAPTER 15

When I got up that morning the sun wasn't shinning as it usually would have been on a day like that in June. *It must gonna be one of those days* I thought to myself. Every now and then the Vegas weather would surprise you. It could be 110° outside and would start sprinkling. Folks would be happy to get that little rain too, but boy when it stopped the sun would beam so hard that if you stood out in it, it would melt your skin. I climbed out of bed and went into the bathroom to wash up. I searched through the closet looking for an outfit for the night. I decided on a jean tennis skirt and sleeveless blue crop top shirt. I packed everything I would need to get ready for the party then I wrapped my hair and showered. I could hear my phone ringing as I tried to wrap the towel around my body. I ran from the bathroom down the hall trying to catch the call before I missed it. I scrolled through the caller ID finding the last number, but it was private. Over the past week someone kept calling me with a private number and I kept missing the call. I waited a second by the phone to see if they would call back, but they didn't. I slipped on the pink sweat shorts and white wife beater then returned to the bathroom to fix my hair. I unwrapped the bandana from around my head and pulled the clips from my hair. I combed my hair down and began to curl the ends with the curling iron. I tilted my head back and brushed the mascara on to my lashes one by one. I took the black eyeliner and lined the inside of my eyes then the upper outside of my eyelids giving myself a cat eye look. I used the eyeliner to line my lips before greasing them up with Vaseline. I dipped my finger in the alcohol bottle and rubbed it around my nose ring. I put the large gold hoop earrings in the first holes of my earlobes and then the ¼ carat diamond studs in the second holes. I arranged the ten gold rings on the fingers they belonged to leaving my thumbs free and wearing two on each of my middle fingers. I slipped the diamond cut rope chain around my neck and walked out the bathroom.

A nice breeze blew threw the open windows. Tifa and I hung black and white streamer threw the apartment while Lacy decorated the table. She placed a large glass punch bowl in the center of the table with stacks of plastic cups on each side. She added plates, napkins and forks to the table and then she taped a black and white balloon on each corner.

"How this look yall" she said, walking towards the stove to check on the chicken.

"Good" we both said shaking our heads yes. "Everything is looking good" Tifa said looking around the newly decorated space. It truly did look good compared to its usual state.

Lacy's mom walked in just as we were admiring our work.

The door slammed hella hard due to all the windows being open mixed with the light breeze. "Ooh y'all I'm sorry, I'm bout to fuck up y'all decorations" she said chasing down the napkins that had blew away from the table. It's ok we said as we tried to keep the balloons and streamer steady from the gust of wind she had brought through. "It's pretty in here" she went on to say as she looked around the clean space.

Lacy pulled a large silver pan from the oven and sat it on the stovetop. She scooped the chicken wings from the frying pan into the silver pan until there was no more in the frying pan. She covered the pan with aluminum foil and placed it back into the oven. "I'm so proud of you baby" Lacy mom said to her as she rubbed her shoulder. "I know you tried to do everything right to graduate and I know you couldn't make it, but baby you tried and I'm happy for that. I'm proud of all of you girls. Please stay beautiful, smart young ladies" she said wiping the tears from her cheeks with one hand and flicking the ashes from her Newport into the ashtray with her other. She went on praising Lacy with love and Birthday wishes. With all Lacy had been through I think she really needed to hear that from her mom. Lacy and her mom wasn't as close as me and my mom or most people and there mom. Lacy didn't get along with her mom mostly because she got high on crack and drank a lot. Once she broke the lock off Lacy's door and took all the change from her mayo jar and on multiple occasions she sold all her food stamps just to buy crack and beer. The last straw for Lacy was the time she left Lacy's baby sister in the house for two hours while she went and smoked crack. After that she and Lacy had a fist fight and Lacy threaten to call CPS if she ever sold another stamp or left one of her siblings alone again. She still smokes crack and drink a lot, but she learned to take care of priorities first. Lacy said she went through the hunger and staying home alone, sleeping in the dark because the lights were cut off all the time when she was little and she wasn't going to let it happen to her younger siblings, not while she was alive. Her siblings really depended on her too, she kept shit in order. She always talked about after graduating she would get her own place and take her siblings with her because she knew after she left her mom would go back to her same old ways of drinking and smoking crack all day. Lacy was planning on going to summer school to get the rest of her credits so she could get her diploma. Her Auntie promised her a job at one of the hotel chains she worked for, but she needed her diploma. She said after she got in good she would hook me and Tifa up with jobs, if we hadn't already had found some. After doing our finishing touches around the house Tifa went home and I walked over to Bombs house to get dress for the party.

CHAPTER 16

I adjusted the jean tennis skirt then slipped on my shoes. I stuffed my dirty clothes into my adidas bag. I gave myself a good look through the mirror that hung behind the bathroom door. I pulled the eyeliner pencil, carmex jar and mascara from my purse. After touching up my mascara and eyeliner I applied a little bit of Vaseline from the carmex jar on to my lips. Turning back to the mirror on the door I practiced a little dance move before opening up the bathroom door and walking out.

Bomb was laying across his bed half asleep when I walked in. when I sat on the bed I could tell it startled him a bit because his body jumped. He opened his eyes and gave me a long blank stare before closing them again. About a minute went by then he slowly raised his self up from the bed. "baby you ok" I said concerned by his unusual body language.

"well damn I had doze off before you come in here jumping on the bed and shit" he said in an irritated voice.

He stretched his arms high in the air and let out a long drawn out yawn. He rubbed his face and head with both his hands before putting the baseball cap on his head. He said he didn't get any sleep last night or the night before and was tired. He apologized for being so snappy after he saw my attitude had quickly changed from happy to mad. The whole time we had been together he had never been mean or disrespectful to me. If we got mad at each other it was usually over something small and it didn't take us long to make back up. He was always sensitive to my feelings. He wasn't like his homeboys. He didn't talk all crazy and call every girl a bitch. He wasn't the type of guy that had to act all macho and put on a show. He was more of the quite type, He was the type that would sit back and observe. He was so different from his brother Deuces. Deuces didn't give a shit about your feelings, and if you couldn't do nothing for him, he wasn't having you around. He wasn't a sugar coater or sweet talker, he always said I'm not hear to make you bitches happy. I often wondered how they came from the same woman, well they did have different daddies. Even though they acted different Bomb did have some of his brother ways especially when it came to his business. Bomb was the weed man on the block. Everybody came to him to buy their halves and ounces. He wasn't a nickel and dime type of dealer. There were a few other scrubs that sold marijuana but it wasn't like bombs. He had that lime green. The kind that Snoop Dogg smoked. It wasn't like that dry crispy Mexican weed with a million seeds. It was fluffy with orange baby buds and it smelled better too.

When we got to the party there were a few people already there. Lacy was in the kitchen putting can sodas in a garbage can she had filled with bags of ice.

"DJ should have been here with the CD's" she said tearing open another bag of ice and pouring it over the can sodas. "Black people always late" she said as she rambled on about how mad she was with him and wasn't going to ask him to DJ anything else for her. He really wasn't late though, we still had 30 minutes before the time we said it would start. "Sorry y'all the music is on its way" she said to the few people standing around waiting. I never understood people showing up early to a party, but there are some that do. Mama always had us a little late to parties. She would say *we have to make a entrance*. Tifa walked in with a hand full of CD's and gave them to Lacy. Lacy put one of the mixed CD's into the CD player and not too long after we had a full house party going on. The later it got the more people showed up. Bomb lit a fat blunt and passed it to me. I puffed it a couple times and passed it backed. Tifa made her way over by us and hit the blunt a few times before disappearing into the crowd. Me and Bomb continued passing the blunt back and forth until it was too short for me to hit then he just finished it off. He kissed my neck and whispered he loved me into my ear as we freaked to the slow jam that was playing. I looked into his eyes and told him I loved him too. Lacy turned on the light and had her cup lifted in the air. "I would like to give toast" she yelled out. "I would like to give a toast" she yelled out again to make sure she had everybody attention. "I just want to say I love all yall, but Fre and Tifa y'all my bitches. Fre when I first met yo ass I couldn't stand you and you knew it cause you couldn't stand me either, probably cause of my mouth" That's right I said as the crowd laughed at the both of us. "but when I got to know you, the real you not that fake stuck up bitch" she said laughing "I knew you was cool and had my back. From that day you've always been there for me when I needed you and I love you girl. Tifa baby we go way back. You like my sista and I love you so much. I'm so happy we here together having this graduation party, even though a bitch didn't graduate. I'm still happy cause my best friends did and I love yall" she said tearing up. All Lacy shut yo crying ass up before you have everybody crying, someone yelled out and the whole room busted out laughing. The lights went back off and the music went back loud. Lacy, Tifa and I shared a long group hug that we continued until we made it outside. Tifa and I told Lacy how much she meant to us also as we stood around the front porch and started to reminisce. "I cant believe we've came this far together yall and now it's over" I said. "What do you mean its over, it's not over" Lacy said. "Well not over, but were finish with school, we bout to be getting jobs and working and having kids and stuff we wont have time no more to just hang out" I said. "Dam really Fre" Tifa said giving me a unhappy stare, the kind I only got from my

mama. "Well shoots that's all I been hearing from mama yall. She makes it like my whole life will be changing over night" I said. "Girl things don't change that fast" Lacy said smiling. Bomb came outside with DJ and West. "Fre we about to walk to the store, you want something" He said.
"Naw I'm cool" I said giving him a kiss on the cheek and watching him walk away with his boys. We went back inside with the party and continued dancing. I went into the kitchen looking for chicken, but I was too late for that. All I found was chicken bones. I poured another drink and stood by the table looking at all the dark silhouettes as they danced, laughed and showed they were having a good time. I saw Deuces had finally showed up. He and Tifa were sitting on the stairs having a good old conversation for the most part they both looked happy. Sometimes I don't know how she does it. To always have to wait around and hope someone shows up or have to wonder if

they're really out hustling or just laid up with the next chic. I don't think I could play anything but first in a relationship. She doesn't seem to mind though and I respect the fact that she still knows how to have a good time wether he's around or not. They both were looking in my direction and laughing so I went over "Hey Deuces" I said. Who yall laughing at I asked smiling because I knew they were laughing at me for some reason. "Hey what up" he said "you over there looking loaded" he said laughing along with Tifa. "Yall out of line laughing at me" I said laughing with them. He had a funny but cute laugh kinda like his brother. I noticed He and Tifa were rocking the same Chuck Taylor's. I knew it was on purpose because they both looked brand new and I had never seen Tifa with that color pair before.

"Hey bro" Lacy said to Deuces when she walked up. I like yall Chucks she went on to say as she admired them and the fact that they had on matching shoes. "I'm bout to walk my lil cousins half way to the bus stop. You want to walk with me" she asked. Talking to me, but I said no because I was waiting for Bomb to come back from the store.

"Girl I might not be here when you get back so give me a hug" Tifa said to Lacy as she stood up. Lacy gave her a look and then looked at me. Tifa knew how Lacy and I felt about Deuces always showing up for a second and her running off with him. "Fre you gonna wait for me to get back" she said waiting on my answer.

As I sat on the stairs I started to watch the last of the party seekers as they continued their groove to the music. Deuces was right I was loaded because I found myself daydreaming. A loud round of gunfire snapped me out of it. At that moment DJ paused the music and it was as silent as a church mouse. I instantly started to panic as Tifa ran through the door falling over herself when another round of gunfire started to erupt. I fell to the floor with my friend as I tried to understand what she was trying to say. "FRE, NO, NO" "LACY" she cried out non stop as people started running out the door to see what happened.

CHAPTER 17

There wasn't a dry eye in the church as the woman sang Amazing Grace. When I was little and went to church with my grama that was my favorite song, but now I only heard it at funerals.

Tifa squeezed my hand tight as to let me know she was still there with me. I sat straight up motionless as tears streamed from both my eyes like watcrfalls.

Tifa signaled for Kleenex from a close by usher. I dropped my head in my lap and balled uncontrollably.

The pastor was halfway through his sermon and I knew it was almost time for me to see Bomb for the last time. I couldn't comprehend the fact that he was gone. Taken from me.

The church was packed from top to bottom. It was silent of talk, but loud with cries when the funeral directors approached the casket and started removing the lay of flowers. Tifa gave me another squeeze of the hand, but this time it felt more as if she needed the strength. I thought about how hard it had to be for her trying to comfort her best friend and also her boyfriend. As Tifa and I walked towards the casket all I could replay in my head was kissing him on the cheek before he walked away with DJ and West that night.

Tifa and I had to put our strength together as we held each other up standing in front of the casket. We took a good moment to say our last goodbye. Walking away from the casket was harder than walking up to it. Deuces stood from the church pew and gave Tifa and I a long warm hug. I could feel all our bodies vibrating together with rumbles of cry.

After the church service we followed the hurst down to the cemetery where Bomb was laid to rest and from there Tifa and I went to her house and changed out of our funeral dresses to our airbrushed R.I.P tshirts and cut off jean shorts. We then went to the projects for the repast that was more like a block party. The streets were filled with people, there to celebrate Bombs home going.

The day after Bombs funeral Tifa and I arrived at the hospital later than we expected to. Since the shooting we had been spending most of our days and nights there by Lacy's side. We both felt guilty not being there with her the day before, but her mom assured us nothing had changed in her health during that time. I stood by her bedside and rubbed the backside of hand staring at her motionless face. Praying to GOD over and over like I had been doing the past 3 weeks. *Please GOD bring my friend out of this coma she doesn't deserve this, she is too young to die, I've lost enough, please I cant loose her too.* I prayed over and over. Most of the time there I stayed quiet and Tifa did most of the talking. She would talk to Lacy as if Lacy could hear her. She told

Lacy all about Bombs funeral down to the part where they lowered him into the ground and both of us throwing a rose onto his casket for her. She told Lacy she couldn't die, she was the strongest of the three of us and how much we needed her.

Lacy was the strong one. She had been through a lot in such a short time. More than the average person would go through in a life time. Being born a crack baby, moving place to place, being left alone hungry with younger siblings she had to care for and now on top of all that being gunned down and trying to hang on to dear life. I couldn't help but shed a tear standing there. Tifa came over to the side of the bed where I was standing and assured me it was going to be ok, but what, what was going to be ok. I already lost Bomb and before that my baby and now my second best friend NO I couldn't loose anything more.

A group of Doctors walked in the room so Tifa and I went out to give them some privacy. We walked down to the cafeteria and picked up a bite to eat. Over the past 3 weeks we had became regulars in the hospital cafeteria. Tifa stretched out across the booth and closed her eyes as I sat across from her and picked at my hamburger and fries. I started to think about Bomb and the last moments we spent together. I often thought if things would have been different if I had just walked to the store with him that night. Would he still be alive or would I be dead with him. Lacy too, I had a chance to be with her also, but I wanted to stay behind and wait for Bomb. Had I just skipped death twice.

I felt guilty for not being there with either of them, what made me stay behind I don't know.

When we returned to Lacy's room nothing had changed but the time on the clock. She still laid there motionless. Her eyes tightly shut, her hair pulled back behind her ears and her body from her chest down covered in a blanket. Her mom sat at her bedside with her head down. She heard us come in but didn't budge. The silence was quiet disturbing not knowing if something had happened while we were gone. Not wanting to ask questions Tifa and I sat there silent until Lacy's mom acknowledged our presence. You girls should go home and get some rest. When she wakes up I will call yall. That was the same line she had repeated to us the past three weeks and that had became our Q that it was time to go and let her be alone with her daughter.

I laid my head on the car window starring out into the dark sky, not a star in sight. *On a day like this GOD could have gave me at least one star to wish upon* I thought to myself. I didn't have to look at Tifa or hear her to know she was crying with me. I could feel it through the complete silence the whole ride to my home. She pulled her car into the driveway and turned off the ignition. She pounded both her fist on the steering

wheel and the beep from the horn startled me.
"I know Tifa" I said repeatedly as she yelled why over and over.
"I know girl" I said as I began to cry to.
We took turns consoling each other for hours in the car as we talked about Bomb and Lacy through memories we had with them. Some good, bad and funny.
Some we told over and over again because they were our favorites. We cried, we laughed, we even sat in more complete silence.

CHAPTER 18

By the time I got to the phone it had stopped ringing. It was a private number so I waited a few minutes to see if they were going to leave a message, but they didn't. I was getting tired of the private numbers with no messages sometimes I even thought it might had been a sign from Bomb checking on me. As I was leaving my room the phone rang again.

"SHIT" I yelled out as I stumped my baby toe on the leg of the bed trying to get to the phone before they hung up.

"Hello"

"Fre"

"Fre,

hey Fre" He said.

My heart sunk in my chest. I felt like the air was being pulled out my chest as he repeatedly called my name.

"Fre" he called again.

"Audi" "um hey Audi" I said

I knew that he could hear the somber in my voice. He told me he had heard about Bomb and Lacy and that he was so sorry. He asked how I was doing and told me to keep my head up it was going to be alright. He told me he had been thinking about me since it all had happened and that he had called multiple times, but no one answered.

I wanted to ask him why he didn't leave a fucking message if he was so concerned, but not because I wanted him too, but because I would have known by now it wasn't Bomb trying to send me messages from heaven.

I sat there listening to him go on and on about how everything was going to be ok. *Who said it was going to be ok* I thought to myself. I hated when people said that. *Everything is going to be ok*. It almost reminded me of when mama says everything happens for a reason. Who comes up with this stuff I thought as I let him go on. After he ran out of stuff to say I thanked him for the call and hung up.

After that day Audi called me everyday. Sometimes I answered sometimes I didn't. It all depended on my mood at the time. If he thought I was home and just wasn't picking up his calls he would call private. I hated when he did that because he would catch me picking up sometimes.

I told him I was still mourning Bomb and he was being a distraction. He claimed that he knew Bomb wouldn't want me sad and would want me to be happy again. He even said if it was him he would want me to be happy. Weeks went by and Audi never missed a day calling me. He had started calling so much until I found myself waiting for his calls. Not because I wanted a relationship with him again, but because he was someone to talk to. During our conversations he did most the talking and I sometimes cried while on the phone with him without him knowing it. By the fifth week he had started telling me he loved me before ending our calls although I would never say it back he still said it.

He eventually started to want to see me, but I didn't want to see him. Something in me wanted to, but I didn't want to. I was mad at myself for even thinking about it. I felt guilty and lonely.

I hadn't heard much from Tifa. At first we were talking like everyday and seeing each other a few times a week, but now she had been spending a lot more time with Deuces and I had been spending most my time at home.

The last few months had been life changing. When you think of life changing you think of something good like someone celebrating a sixteenth birthday, a graduation, a baby being born or a marriage. You don't think of Death and a coma. I didn't. Truth was death had started lingering around and it wasn't going anywhere no time soon. Some nights I would lay there for hours staring up at the ceiling fan Watching it spend round and round as thoughts of bomb spend round and round in my head. Sometimes I would run down our whole relationship in my mind. I thought about it all From our first slow dance to our last, the first movie we saw together, the times we spent by the pond and making love in the back seat of his brothers car. Everyday I missed him more and more.

CHAPTER 19

Lacy came out of her coma, but they said she would never have a normal life. Her mom decided to send her down south with her Aunt Bee who had money, a big house, lots of land and more than enough room to accommodate Lacy and the ongoing care she would need. Lacy had told us about her Aunt Bee, she use to live with her for a short time when she was about 9 or 10. She always had good stuff to say about her Aunt Bee, but couldn't stand Aunt Bee's husband Charleston. She once told us when she lived with them he made late night visits to her room on many occasions. Once Lacy's mom had the younger children Aunt Bee wanted to send for them over summer break, but Lacy wouldn't let them go. She always made up a reason why they couldn't go. I don't think she ever told anyone about uncle Charleston except Tifa and I. I always wondered how someone could keep a secret like that from their mother. She didn't seem too embarrassed by it either when telling us, but that was like Lacy it was a lot she could have been embarrassed about that she wasn't. Her life was like a open book and a lesson to be learned. The stuff she went through seemed to make her stronger. I sat on the edge of the queen size bed looking around the studio apartment. It was a very small place but big enough for its purpose. I hadn't seen Tifa in months. She had been spending all her time with Deuces and I had thought about going over to Lois house, but that meant I would have to be in a place where Bomb was suppose to be. Where he use to sleep, eat, laugh. Live. Deuces had been in the spot a little over two weeks and Tifa had been trying to get me over there the whole time. I had finally made it after too many times of not showing up when I said I would. Tifa passed me the blunt and told me to hit it, it would make me feel better. I never said I didn't feel good, but I guess my expression told it all. It was like my first time really getting out the house and actually hanging out since Bomb had died and she was right I did need it. We passed the blunt back and forth to each other until it was too short to hit. Deuces came in and seemed a little shocked to see me. "Hey brother" I said as I got up from the end of the bed and gave him a hug. You could feel the emotions running during our short embrace.

"How you been Fre" he asked

"I've been ok I guess" I said hoping he knew how much I really missed his brother and wasn't really ok at all. I was still mourning his death. He grabbed a small brown glass jar from the freezer and sat at the table that was placed in the center of the room. He took a half smoked blunt from the ashtray and dipped it in the small brown glass jar. The odor kinda threw me for a loop. It was a strong chemically smell that I had never smelled before. He lit the now wet blunt and over a short period of time his attitude started to change. He turned up the radio and began to grind on Tifa. She started grinding back and before you knew it they was up dancing in the small space. Their happiness made me smile. I hadn't smile and meant it since Bomb was alive. Thinking about him in that instant made me sad all over again. There was a knock at the door. Deuces lowered the radio and looked out the peephole.

"Who is it" he said

"Twenty" they yelled back through the door. He opened it and made a quick transaction before closing the door back. He turned back up the radio and finished grinding with Tifa. I didn't know what to make of Tifa and Deuces relationship especially the way it had started. Until then I hadn't thought of it as one, but after spending time with them I realized they had something there. I was happy for her, but envious that I no longer had happiness. I could feel myself instantly get sick to the stomach and breakout in sweat.

"Fre girl you ok" Tifa said

As she stood hovered over me with both her hands placed on my shoulders. The stare she was giving me had been there longer than I thought.

"I'm good" I said

As I tried to remember the last thing we were talking about before I blanked out.

"you sure you ok"

she asked again with deep concern

"I'm sure girl" I said while trying to get her to leave it alone. I got up and walked into the bathroom. Standing there staring at myself through the mirror, my eyes filled with water. I gasped for a breath of air and the tears poured from my eyes as the air escaped my body. I bent over with my head in the sink and splashed cold water over my face. My tears and snot mixing with water as I continuously splashed the water over my face. I took the towel hanging from the towel rack and wiped my face dry. For the next three weeks I had not seen the light of day or anybody, but my mom and brother. I tried to avoid all phone calls and I spent all day and night locked up in my room. The only time I left it was for food and the bathroom. My mom didn't notice how depress I had became because she was at work most of the day and by the time she got home I would act like I was just getting in the bed, but really I had been there all day. She asked on occasions about Tifa and sometimes I would act like I had been with her earlier in the day. I hid my feelings well but not well enough for myself. Over time I had gotten tired of the way I was feeling. I realized no amount of tears was going to bring him back. The phone rang so much that day I had no choice but to unplug it from the wall. I turned the radio on and they were playing slow jams. I pushed back colorful striped curtains and raised the blinds. I opened the window and was hit in the face by a cool breeze of fresh air. I stood there with my eyes closed letting the rays from the sun and waves of cool air cleanse my body and mind of darkness. I turned the volume all the way up on my boombox and started singing to all the songs that played back to back. I stripped my bed of the sheets and replaced them with new ones. I picked up all the trash that had started to pile up and had begun to give the room a foul odor. I hung up the clothes that had found a home in one of the corners of my room. I found a vase from under the kitchen sink and placed the flowers from Bomb casket in it and placed it on the night stand next to my bed. I tacked his obituary on the wall over my headboard. I pulled up my large rug took it outside and shook all the dust off. I vacuumed the floor and replaced the rug. I laid across my neatly made bed looking around the room making sure everything was in it's place. I noticed the phone and plugged it back into the wall. It wasn't five minutes before it started ringing. I picked up on the second ring. It wasn't a surprise that it was Audi. It would have been more of a surprise if it wasn't. He called with his usual talk. How you doing? What you doing? Have you eaten? Are you alright? My answer never changed until he asked if he could come see me. It had been no the last few months but then I said yes.

CHAPTER 20

Audi and I had been hanging out everyday since I had said yes to seeing him. We were seeing two to three movies a week, going out to eat, and spending late nights at the park watching the sunrise. Without either one of us saying it we were a couple again and it seemed like everything had fallen back in place from where it had left off when we were on good terms. Way before the abortion and way before Samantha came along and broke us apart.

Time seemed like it had flew by. It was already fall and I couldn't help but to think about how summer had came and gone, taking away so much with it. We often sat and reminisced about the good times which always seemed to bring up the bad ones in my mind. Some days I questioned myself as to if I had made the right decision getting back involved with Audi after all that had happened. The abortion, him cheating with

Samantha, the breakup, Lacy getting shot and Bomb getting killed. It was all so much to deal with and all so fast. I begged God for a reason why, why all of this.

After being home that summer Audi had no intention on going back to school. I questioned if it had anything to do with me but he kept telling me the decision had been made months prior to him coming home and was mainly because of his parents getting divorced. He was a true mamas boy and he couldn't stand being that far away from his mom especially at a time when he thought she really needed him. She was against him coming home, but he insisted and promised to enroll for classes at the community college. Mrs. Tate had been living with her sister and Audi decided to stay in the house with his dad. He was upset that his mom had left her home and thought she should have made his dad leave, but she said when he left for college she couldn't stand being in the house alone and that's why she moved in with her sister. She was waiting for the divorce to be finalized and was planning on buying herself a small condo. Audi made sure his dad felt his presence back in the house and made sure he didn't have any lady friends in the house he and his mom once shared.

The absents of a woman was clearly noticeable. The cleanness of the place was diminishing with each visit and you could tell love didn't live there anymore.

Dishes were piled up in the sink. The kitchen floor hadn't been mopped in awhile. There were piles of clothes that made there way from the dryer right to the couch and no further. The ironing board had been up in the living room for days and no telling how long it had been since the carpet had been vacuumed. Mr. Tate was never really home which gave Audi and I the house to ourselves. We had gotten use to being with each other 24/7.

Since I had been there so much I decided to

cleanup the place. I turned on the tv and found the music channel. Once Audi saw what I was doing he quickly jumped in and started to help. Neither one of us heard his dad come through the door because of the loud vacuum cleaner running and R&B blasting from the tv.

He excused himself as he tip toed over the neatly vacuumed carpet into the kitchen area. As much as I hated his father I couldn't be rude and disrespectful in his house so I turned the vacuum cleaner off to hear him speak. He seemed to have been in a good mood trying to hold a conversation with Audi about how bad the house needed some TLC and how his mother would have had a fit if she saw it in the previous state. He even thanked me and tried making small talk. He pulled forty from his wallet and asked Audi to order a couple of pizzas. He asked me what I liked on my pizza and told Audi to make sure he got what I liked. *REALLY, what do I like on my pizza fuck a pizza.* I thought to myself as I thanked him and finished up the carpet. I use to like Mr.Tate way before I found out he played a part in the decision of our child and way before I found out he cheated on Mrs.Tate. I use to think of him as the man I wished my father was. Come to find out he was no saint, no different than my father. I started to wonder if the sayings about men were true. Were they all cheaters, dogs, weak when it came to a woman. Is it something in the gene of a man that makes them so easily subdued by a woman. A man could have it all from lots of money, beautiful wife, kids, big home and still will risk it all in one night on some ass. It must be in the genes.

CHAPTER 21

I had less than twenty minutes to make it downtown for my interview at the Hamburger Spot. Audi had got a job there and after finding out they were short staff he brought me an application to fill out. Mama offered me a ride to the interview since she had called earlier talking my ear off about her brother not returning the money he had borrowed from her months ago. She should have known she wasn't going to get it back because she never got it back from any of them when she loaned them cash. I was waiting outside when she pulled up and I practically ran towards the car, slung open the door and jumped in the front passenger seat before she could come to a complete stop.

"Hey mama" I said staring at her with a big smile. I was really happy to see her. I hadn't seen her in awhile and the last time I did it was for a brief moment. I talked with her almost everyday just to check in and let her know I was ok though.

"Girl you gonna let me stop the car first" she said smiling back as she continued down the road. She talked the whole way there. She first started with my uncle not returning the money like he promised and then about how she was mad that Mani had been spending more time at his dads house. "I know it's because his stepbrothers are there but my goodness" she said in agony. "And you missy, you too just stay gone. Y'all will have people thinking I just gave my kids away" she kept going on. "Those folks probably tired of looking at you everyday" she carried on with more jibber jabber as I quickly tuned her out thinking about the job interview and the type of questions they might ask me.

"So how do you know Mr. Tate" was the first question the manager asked. Good thing Audi had already warned me not to say we were a couple just in case they were the type of company that didn't hire kinfolks and friends.

"We went to school together" I said like it was nothing else to it. She asked a few more questions, some more personal than others but by the time the interview was over I had the job.

Working at the Hamburger Spot was cool besides the fact that Audi and I had different shifts. He worked mornings 9am to 5pm and I worked evening 3pm to 10pm. On weekends we had the same shift 8am to 4pm which was good because Mr.Tate either drove us or he would let Audi use the car. It wasn't long before all the staff found out Audi and I were a couple. Just so happened on one of the weekends we were working together, a group of dudes came in clowning. One of the guys started to flirt with me and after I rejected to giving him my number he started calling me all out of my name. Audi warned the guy to cut it out, telling him if he kept talking to me like that he would have to leave. The guy kept going on and with the help of his friend instigating it he became more vulgar with his language towards me and added some choice words for Audi.

"All you ole captain save a hoe ass nigga" the guy said pointing his finger in Audi's face

"Nigga you beta watch yo mouth and get the fuck outta here real quick talkin bout my girl, she ain't no hoe" Audi yelled in the guys face.

His arm flew up, and his fist was close to connecting to the guys chin before Marcos pulled Audi back towards the fryer and demanded the guys leave, telling them he called the police and they were on their way. Audi was pissed at Marcos for holding him back. Warning him to never hold him back from kicking someone's ass again.

"Bro I just didn't want you to get fired or even go to jail over some stupid ass youngsta trying to be cool" Marcos explained.

"Man I ain't trippin, but if I see that youngsta in the streets ima stomp his ass out" Audi said with a mischievous grin on his face.

That's the main reason why they don't like hiring family and friends I thought to myself.

After that day we didn't have to worry about hiding our relationship any longer because everyone had known now. Either they worked that shift and were there to witness the commotion or they heard about it from Marcos who made sure to tell the story to everyone who didn't get to witness it. It was actually a relief that we didn't have to hide our relationship anymore, although it didn't change much, it wasn't like we were now making out at the register, It was just the fact of me not being able to say "that's my man" to the females who came into the restaurant flirting with Audi. Before they would get a stank eye along with their shortage of fries, now they get the stank eye, shortage of fries and me yelling to Audi "babe her order is up" with my own mischievous grin.

CHAPTER 22

Marcos invited Audi and I to his house one Saturday after work, it was not an actual house, but an attached apartment to a duplex that he shared with other family members. He, his mother, three sisters and auntie stayed in one of the upstairs units and next door was another one of his aunties, uncle and their four children. Down below in one unit was his Grandparents and next door to them were more relatives cousins and such. Each unit only had two bedrooms and one bathroom. As I looked around the small space I tried to figure out in my head how all of them could possibly live there together. It looked as if Marcos had his room all to his self so I guess that meant the girls had the other room, then where did that leave his mother and auntie. Maybe the sofa in the living room was also a bed I thought to myself. The three sisters seemed close in age, all looking around fourteen or fifteen.

They favored each other so much they could have passed as triplets. They all had long thick wavy black hair that went pass their butts, big dark brown eyes and olive colored skin. The only thing that was noticeably different was their attitudes.

As I watched the sisters interact with one-another I thought about how it would have been to have had a sister of my own. I had always wanted a sister. Someone close in age I could have grown up with and share my deepest secrets with, someone I could have told anything too and she wouldn't have judged me, someone to share clothes with, talk about boys with, party with. Someone who would love me for me no matter what. Tifa and Lacy was the closest I got to having sisters and in that moment I realized how lucky I was to have them. Folks always talked about how hard it was to find a genuine friend and I can say I had two. Although people knew I considered both Tifa and Lacy as my best friends, they still thought I liked Tifa more. Some would even say " you can't have two best friends" but that was a lie I always told them. I can have whatever I want.

One of the sisters turned the volume up on the stereo and started dancing. She swung her hips side to side in a fast moving motion that her feet could barely keep up with. She began singing and walking closer to her sisters, grabbing both of them by the arms, pulling them up from the sofa to join her. One jumped right in singing and moving her hips just as fast to the music. The other one covered her face with her hands and ran back to the sofa plopping down next to me in laughter.

"why you not going to dance" I asked her "because she shy" one of the sisters yelled in her face.

The other two sisters kept on dancing and singing without missing a beat or note. They were dam good too. I couldn't believe how good they danced to the salsa music. With

their looks and age I know they could have made some money if they started a girl group. It was like triple J Lo.
"You guys are good" I said as I continued to watch the girls. The shy sister finally jumped up and joined in after hearing all the praise I was giving out to her sisters. I could tell singing and dancing was something they did together on a regular by the number of choreograph moves they had and when singing they made sure not to jump in each other's part of the song.
All three girls came and pulled me up off the couch to join them in a salsa dance. I couldn't understand the music but after watching long enough I caught on to the dance moves. We spent a good while having fun, dancing, singing and crying with laughter. By the time we stopped I felt like I had just finished a workout.

CHAPTER 23

Walking into Marcos room was like walking through a foggy forest. The marijuana smoke along with the pine tree air freshener smell filled every square inch of the small room. Audi took a hit of the blunt and passed it my direction. I was shocked to see him smoking, but happy at the same time because I hadn't smoke since the last visit I had with Tifa and I was over due. It felt a little awkward for me to be smoking around Audi. It even brought back memories of me and Bomb. Anytime Bomb and I would smoke with other people, he would pass the blunt to me, I hit it and pass it back to him, he hit it and pass it to the next person. He didn't care about fucking up the rotation and when his homies talked shit he would say my girl ain't hittin the blunt after you niggas and you niggas ain't hittin the blunt after my girl. It started after one of his homies complimented me on the taste and smell of my peach lip gloss. Bomb was close to kicking his ass, but it was just us three so he gave him a pass. I hit the blunt once and passed it to Marcos. I didn't want Audi to learn at that moment how experience I had become to smoking weed. Not that he could say anything about it, especially after me seeing him toke up. It's just in the past we both talked bad about people who smoked, especially females. But now I was one of them, we were both one of them. I didn't care though I liked the feeling. Looking at Audi I started to wonder how much weed had he smoked since our breakup because he wasn't smoking like a amateur, as a matter of fact we could have been on the same level except I just wasn't showing my true level at the moment. After dumbing the long grey ash into the ashtray he passed the blunt to me. That time I hit it twice and held it in a few extra seconds before lifting my head and blowing the cloud of smoke up in the air, watching it join the already clouds of smoke chilling at the ceiling of the room. Two of Marcos cousin busted in the room both laughing at something or someone they were trying to escape from. Closing the door quickly behind them, either to not let out all the weed smell or because of the person who could have been behind them.

"I knew I smelled some bomb" one of the cousin said as he grabbed the doobie steadily from Marcos fingers trying not to drop it.

"Go ahead kill it, I'm about to roll another one" Marcos said.

My heart dropped after somebody started banging at the door so hard you'd thought it was the police.

I know you in there hijo de puta, ima patea tu culo.
The woman screamed from the other side of the door. Marcos swung the door open. The woman was screaming something in Spanish as she tried pushing herself through the door but couldn't fight pass Marcos 300 lb. solid body
"Tia, chill out man,
what's el problema" he said
as he tried calming his auntie down while his two cousin cried with laughter.
"Tia come in and hit the blunt,
you need to calm down" he said
pulling her in and closing the door behind them.
"Dis hijo de puta's are so jodidamente estùpido Marcos,
why, why….". She cried
as she continued cursing them in Spanish mixed with a little English like most Mexicans do when they're really mad. I

wish I had learned more Spanish in my Spanish 1 class, but I just couldn't get it. All I knew was papas fritas, hola come estas, uno, dos, tres, cuatro, cinco, seis, siete, ocho, nueve, dies, and a few curse words. I still don't know what they did to her, but she finally calmed down after hitting the blunt and by the time it went into a full rotation she was laughing, but still cursing them. For whatever the reason was I thought her initial reaction was a little over the top, but I was glad to see it wasn't too serious. *And they say black women are crazy*, I thought to myself.

CHAPTER 24

I learned that Tia was Marcos auntie who lived with them. She was just a few years older than he was and since they were so close in age and grew up together they were more like brother and sister. Tia was shorter than most girls her age and on the chubby side. She had long black hair like Marcos little sisters did, but hers didn't fit her the same way. It was extremely too long for her being so short, it made her look like Cousin It from the movie. Her face was evenly rounded and she had big roses cheeks that matched her lips, but was all natural no makeup except heavy eyeliner and mascara. If you looked at her long enough you could find cute qualities about her. She was a feisty little thing which made her cuter and probably turned guys on. Marcos mother had practically raised her and his two cousins who I found out were twins. No one could ever guess that because they looked totally opposite. When they came running in the room laughing that day, I could tell they might had been brothers because they laughed the same way, both covered their mouths with their fist. Even when they talked they sounded exactly alike and I caught them finishing a few of each other sentences, but I would have never ever guessed twins. Obviously they were fraternal twins, but still twins always amazed me. They're names were Jesus and Jose, but I heard everyone calling both of them J. At one time Marcos addressed Jose as small J I'm sure it was because he was the short twin. He stood about 5'3 and couldn't have weighed no more than 150 lbs soak and wet. He wore a Caesar style haircut, and had thick black eyebrows that almost made a unibrow. His lips were also a red rose color, naturally. In fact looked like the whole family was blessed with those lips. The only facial hair he had to go along with those thick eyebrows was a thin mustache that I thought he could have done without. His twin brother on the other hand was taller, he also had the thick eyebrows but no mustache and his hair was long and pulled back into a ponytail. His texture matched Marcos little sisters and aunt Tia, but he had half their length. He had a nose piercing and a small NY tattoo at the corner of his left eye. You know there's those questions that everybody ask when they meet twins and some who just decide on their own. Who's the cute twin, Who's the bad twin, who's the nice twin, who's the fun twin and so on. I decided for myself Jesus was the cute twin and I'm sure the bad and fun one too. Jose seemed more like the nice pretty boy type as where Jesus had those rough edges around him. The more time

I spent around the both of them I started to notice the qualities they shared and the ones they didn't share. As first suspected Jose was definitely a pretty boy. He stayed clean from head to toe. Anytime you saw him he had on a long crisp white T with black 501 Levi's jeans and all white Air Force One Nike tennis shoes. He kept a fresh haircut with a clean lineup and baby bottom smooth shaved face besides the mini mustache, and I could tell he groomed his unibrow. His attitude sucked but his brothers was no better so that right there was a shared quality for sure. Jesus was more laid back, didn't talk as much as Jose nor did he play as much as him either. Jose was a prankster but most of the time the shit he would pull would make you want to kill him not laugh at the situation. I'm sure it was all him that pissed Tia off when I first met them. Jose would have been Lacy's type of guy. Even though

Tifa always had first dibs on picking the tag alongs I would have made sure to introduce Lacy to Jose first. She loved the pretty boys because she could control them a little easier. She always would say she's too hood for a hood boy and it was nothing but the truth. I can't tell you how many boys she has had to put her hands on. If they had too much hood in them she might not be here to tell it. If Tifa had the choice she would have picked Jesus anyway, for having the ponytail alone would have got him some ass. That girl was a sucka for dudes with long hair. She could spot the back of a guy with hair and before even seeing his face she's already turned on. Once we got a good laugh behind her and her mane pickings we called it. All we saw was this long straight ponytail swaying side to side as we followed it up and down the grocery store isles. She always found a way to make some type of conversation so when she yelled excuse me can you reach this. The woman turned around, yes mama I got it for you, she said, looking Tifa up and down with flirty eyes and as if she knew we had been following her. The woman tried spitting a little game to Tifa but Tifa just apologized and said she wasn't into women. Once we got out of the store Lacy and I laughed until we cried. Anytime it came up or something reminded us of it we still laughed until we cried. Tifa made us promise not to tell anyone and til this day I hadn't, but it still made good as a inside joke whenever I thought about it.

CHAPTER 25

I hadn't been back to see Tifa since my first
visit to her and Deuces new place, but I had
spoke with her on multiple occasions and
kept telling her I would come and see her.
I told her about Audi and I hooking back up,
but made her promise not to mention it to
Deuces. I didn't know how he would react
to me dating so soon after his brothers death
and if it made it worse that it was my ex. I
didn't know if he would or even could
understand how sad and empty I felt without
his brother and how lonely I had become.
Was he even aware that out of the few
people I thought I'd always have by my
side, one of them was now living life like a
vegetable and he had the other one, leaving
me with nothing. I felt like I had lost three
people that I loved all at once.
So, so what if I'm back with my ex.

What did people expect anyway, he was my first love and we did almost share a child so it shouldn't have been a big surprise.

I didn't know why God had put Audi back in my life, after all we had went through, did he really think I could take another round. Don't get me wrong we had the almost perfect relationship, with one major hiccup, that bitch Samantha, shit if it wasn't for her I might have never been with Bomb, I wouldn't have had a reason to be with him or even had known him, like I did.

If it wasn't for her I would have just continued to only have known of him, Bomb from the projects with the brother Deuces, but now he's my lost love, never to be found. No matter how hard I prayed and cried for God to send him back, I knew he was gone forever there was no coming back. Nightly visits in my dreams was the closest I would ever get to seeing him again and the memories I've tucked safely away in my heart was the closest I would ever get to feeling him again.

I kept telling myself if Audi hadn't cheated on me with Samantha this wouldn't have happened, I would have never been with Bomb and never would have had to deal with the heartbreak and loss of him, but I knew that was a lie and if I blamed him I'd have to blame myself because I could have just taken him back and not been with Bomb. I don't know why God had place Bomb in my path, and for such a short time, but like mama always said, everything happens for a reason.

CHAPTER 26

I was happy about the direction Audi and I relationship had started to go. We both were working and started talking about getting a place together. I was still spending a lot of time at his house, but also spending time back at home too. Especially when he, Marcos and the twins would go out because I knew it meant they would be out all night. Audi had become pretty tight with all three of them and they were all hanging tuff on a daily basis. When Audi wasn't at work he was hanging at Marcos, when Marcos was at work Audi would still be at Marcos. With all the family in the same block, it was always something going on around there and always people hanging out. With Marcos, the twins, Tia, Marcos little sisters and friends of everyone it was always a packed yard. It kinda reminded me of the projects. It even had drug transactions going on by the storage room on the side of the building. I peeped Jesus signaling crackheads to that direction whenever they would try walking thru the front gate. I'm sure it was because he didn't want them walking pass his grandparents apartment to get to his door. Although I hadn't seen him physically sell anything I knew it was crack cocaine by the way the customers looked. The ones who came up to buy weed, Marcos took them into his room where he had pounds of weed that I had physically saw with my own eyes. I had never saw that much weed at one time in my life. The most Bomb ever had was two of those ziplock freezer bags full and I thought that was a lot of weed until I saw Marcos stash. I wasn't mad at Audi for hanging with Marcos as much as he did, I just got mad when he made plans to go over there without asking if I wanted to do something else first or when he didn't answer his phone if I called. I could be at work all day and as soon as I get off and call he wouldn't answer and that would burn me up inside, like I been working all day and you can't make yourself available for when I get off, I couldn't understand it.

When I thought about the way Audi was when I first met him. He was a true pretty boy not like Jose, but Kappa Alpha Psi fine. I mean everything about him was pretty. His smile, his eyes although they weren't that odd green color that everyone thought was pretty, the shape of them were pretty along with his eyelashes. He also had a slim physique packed with muscles. He stayed dressed in the best clothes Polo, Tommy Hilfiger, basketball jerseys and all. He was so romantic too. He once snuck up behind me and draped my neck with a gold chain that had a angel hanging from it. I threw away a lot of stuff from our breakup but that was one of the things I kept. I didn't wear it while I was with Bomb because I didn't feel like lying about where I got it, I could have just not said anything but it was one of those things people always thought was pretty and would ask me where I got it. He would always surprise me with little gifts for no reason at all. He would take me everywhere, to every movie, carnival, restaurant, everywhere. Our relationship was fine for all that we had went through together and personally, but we both were different people now. We were smoking weed and drinking Hennessy everyday and he had started selling weed. Not long after that he started pushing dope with Jesus. He finally quit his job at the Hamburger Spot, but me and Marcos was still there. I wondered why Marcos needed a job with all the weed he had. I found out he was on probation and had to keep a job to stay out of jail. I needed my job. There were night I stayed out a little too late knowing I had to get up and go to work the next morning, Audi would talk me into call in. I did it once too many times and got written up. He really wanted me to quit, he kept telling me he made enough to pay my phone bill and give me shopping money, but I couldn't. I liked having my own money plus what would I tell mama. I quit my job and Audi was going to take care of me with his drug money. She knew he wasn't working there no more from the few times she had picked me up and stopped seeing him there. I couldn't lie, I was just not a good lier. If she came out and asked if he was a dealer I probably would say yeah because I hated lying. I wasn't a good lier so why try.

CHAPTER 27

When I finally saw Tifa I was shocked. It looked like she had put on about ten pounds. She had on a white wife beater and some jean shorts that had the butterfly type of buttons which all were unbutton besides the very last one exposing a little round pudge of belly.

"You pregnant" I said squeezing her with a big hug.

I couldn't believe she was pregnant.

I sat and listened as she told me in detail how she just knew the very night it happened when Deuces came in her and her baby was made and how the baby would be born close to his daddy birthday, maybe even on it if he happened to come two weeks early. She told me how happy Deuces was when he saw the pregnancy test and she described how he held it in the sky waving it

like a wand screaming this my lil nigga. Her eyes lit up more and more with every new detail that spilled from her mouth as tears were preparing to spill from my eyes.
"Oh Fre"
she said moving closer to me.
"I'm so sor" she said before I cut her off.
"Girl stop what you sorry for I'm about to cry cause I'm happy for y'all, shit ima be a auntie" I said wiping the tears from both my eyes with the palms of my hands.
"So what else been going on" I said. Giving her the permission she needed to continue. If she knew for any second that I was crying for my own personal reason and not because I was so happy to be an aunt, she would have not said another word about the baby, but that's not what I wanted. I was very happy for Tifa, just taken by surprise.
"I went shopping for baby clothes, we don't know what it is yet, I'm only eleven weeks, so I just got stuff that can be for a boy or girl" she said grabbing some bags from the

side of the couch.
I don't know why when women find out they pregnant, they just have to go buy something for the baby.
It's like a way to signify your pregnancy and welcome the baby into the home before it's really in the home, a way to show it has its place there, room, bed, clothes, food and parents. She pulled each item from the bags one by one. The bibs read stuff like worlds cutest baby, mommy's baby, if you think I'm cute you should see my daddy and My Grandma loves me. The outfits were my favorite. She bought two Air Jordan onesie with matching booties, one in grey and white the other in red and black. I got more excited as she continued pulling stuff out of the bags, everything was just so little and cute. By the time she finished showing me everything, that baby could wear a new outfit everyday of his first thirty days of life. As she sat on the floor, folding each item and placing it back in a bag, she directed the

attention on me.

"So what's been up with you" she asked in a slow cautious way.

I don't know what my big smile told her, but she started smiling just as hard.

"W-e-l-l, I told you I got back with Audi"
I said then paused.

"Ye-a-h-h-h",
she said slowly and sarcastically mimicking my slow response.

After rehearsing over and over in my head on how I was going to tell her face to face, when the time came I still got stuck with a mouth full of speechless words.

"Fre
it's ok...,
that's good"
she quickly said after noticing the shame written all over my face, lifting herself from the floor and taking a seat right next to me.

"Fre hunny, it's ok,
we know you loved Bomb,
and girl...

I know how much you love Audi, that nigga
is yo first love and y'all then been through
thick and thin, shor.
y'all almost made me a tee tee first.
Look I know you, and I know you aww
worried about what people gone think, but
fuck them. Can't nobody tell you how you
should feel or what you should do in a
situation like this, nobody but God.
Sis Bomb is gone and I know you miss him,
everyday,
we all do,
but… you still have a heart, so save a piece
of your heart for him, but continue to use the
rest of your heart.
I love you"
she said pulling me into her arms and
squeezing me tight.
I stayed a little while longer as we took turns
catching each other up on everything that
had been happening in our lives. I told her
how Audi and I had been smoking like a
train and drinking like fish and how I tried

to play it off acting like I didn't really smoke weed our first time getting high together.

He eventually called me out on it. I told her about us both working at The Hamburger Spot and how Audi didn't work there anymore because he was now making way more money selling dope, she couldn't believe that part.

"My bro a dough boy, and you thought you had a pretty boy"

she laughed, while still expressing how she couldn't believe it. I was happy when she called him her bro, it felt just like one of our old time conversations. She joked saying that when Mr. and Mrs. Tate found out, they were going to kick his ass. We both cracked up because we knew it was true, this would give Mrs. Tate a whole heart attack. She would probably just blame it on Mr. Tate though, as something else bad behind their sour breakup, he wouldn't have came home from college if they hadn't broken up, she thought. Audi hated being the only child. He always said it was too much attention, too much trying to protect him. He admitted he liked all the attention when he was younger. They spoiled him rotten for being the only child, and Mrs. Tate felt guilty for not being able to give him a sibling. It was hard enough for her giving birth to him, for a long time she thought she couldn't have kids and all of a sudden It happened, but with high risks and that's when the doctors told her it would be safe to not have anymore or else she could die. That's why she spoiled Audi the way she did and I'm sure he liked being spoiled, what kid wouldn't. He said up until he was like nine his parents couldn't do anything without him, not even go on a dinner date without him. He also admitted thats the age he realized he was fucking up his pops quality time with his mama. He realized they could be out having fun, dancing, enjoying each other and during that time he could be doing some shit of his own.

Everyone was happy but his mama. She thought her baby was growing up too fast, wanting to stay home alone while they went out. I'm sure that's when he discovered a lot about his parents. When the cats away the mice will play, and play is what he did. Rummaging through his parents shit. He found where Mr. Tate kept his guns, he found a sack of weed and rolling papers in their top drawer. He remembered the mysterious yellow chest that Mrs. Tate kept under her side of the bed. He opened that and discovered porno tapes, dildos and assortments of lubes and creams. I always died laughing at the stories he told me about his childhood and the shit he got away with, being the only child. Tifa could somewhat relate to Audi about being the only child because she too was a only child, she just didn't have her parents around, but she knew all about being spoiled rotten and getting pretty much anything she wanted.

CHAPTER 28

Tifa asked me to go with her to her doctor appointment and I couldn't say no, especially since she was there for me when I needed her. I held her hand while the nurse rubbed her belly down with the clear ultrasound gel and used the wand to search for the baby's heartbeat. The sound of it put a smile on both of our faces. Tifa really wanted to know if she was having a boy or girl but it was still too early to tell. I'm sure Deuces would be with her for that appointment. He of course was hoping for a baby boy and Tifa was hoping for a baby girl, but most of all a healthy baby. She had all her appointment lined up. She had so many appointment she had to buy one of those small pocket calendar just to remember them all. First she had to go down to the welfare office and take them proof of pregnancy so she could get a medical card, food stamps, and cash benefits. Then she had to go down to the office and start her W.I.C which provided her with milk, cheese, cereal, peanut butter and a few other things. Then once she had the baby they would provide her with baby formula on top of the other stuff. Then she had a appointment for the housing program that would place her in a low income apartment which would be in one of the many projects around town. You didn't have much choice of where you wanted to live it pretty much went by what was available at the time your name came up on the list. You could take it or leave it, if you were smart you were taking it. Who wouldn't want almost free rent. Since it was based on your income you'd have some folks paying ten dollars, some five, some just two and some nothing at all. It was good they had programs like housing, W.I.C, and welfare to help women with kids. I didn't mind going with Tifa to her doctor appointments, but I was not trying to spend none of my days in a welfare or W.I.C office. There was always way too many people, not enough seats and snotty nose children running around everywhere.

She had one more regular doctor appointment before finding out the gender so I promised her I would go with her to that appointment.

When I stopped and thought about it, I couldn't help but laugh at how backwards things had became.

The life Tifa was living was suppose to be my life, I was the one who should have been planning the arrival of a baby. Tifa never wanted kids, she was the one who said she'll never settle down, the one who thought she could never have a man of her own, not because she couldn't get one, but because she couldn't see herself tied down with one. She never had a steady relationship like I had, all the guys she dated belonged to another girl and she was always the side chick, but like I said she preferred it that way, that was until Deuces came along, he was the one man she wanted for herself. Love at first sight in her eyes. I honestly have to say I never thought in my wildest dreams that they could be together. Being that Deuces was much older and all, I just couldn't see it happening. Just like I couldn't see a lot of other things happening but they happened. Lacy also never talked about having kids but it wasn't because she didn't want them, it was more because she thought she would always be the one who looked out for her younger siblings and by the time they all grew up she'd be too old to think about kids of her own. She had boyfriends here and there but never nothing serious. I was the friend always tied down in a relationship and the one who was most likely to have the kids and live the family life. I cracked up inside at how fucking humorous my life was at that moment.

When I thought I had life figured out, I could just say what will happen and thought that's how it was going to be. So immature to adulthood.

CHAPTER 29

Audi picked me up from work with Marcos who hadn't been to work in the past three days. I was pissed off with him because I had to cover one of his days on my day off. He tried speaking to me as he got out the front passenger seat of the car, I rolled my eyes as I plopped down on the seat and slammed the car door. I turned to Audi and started yelling at him for arriving late. He tried calming me down, but I was steaming mad. "First you pick me up late, and you bring somebody with you" I yelled.
"If you mad I'll just drop you off at home" he said.
"You ain't dropping me off no fucking were" I responded, crossing my arms and facing the passenger window. *He was not dropping me off nowhere, wherever he was*

going I was going.
We rode around the town making stops in different neighborhoods. We stopped by the mini mart to pickup a bottle of Hennessy and a swisher sweet.

When we arrived at Marcos house his twin cousins were already in there waiting. "Man what took y'all fools so long" Jose asked as soon as we walked inside. Jesus was sitting at the kitchen table cutting up crack cocaine. Audi grabbed a seat at the table and pulled two bags from his pocket each carrying a large solid white rock of cocaine. He tore open one of the bags dropping the solid chalk like object on to the plate sitting in front of him. He took a razor blade and sliced into the rock. It broke into 3 chunks leaving little chips of it laying around. He then took the razor and sliced each of the three chunks into teeth size pieces. After working with the first rock he placed all the pieces into one baggie then moved on to the next large white rock of crack cocaine, repeating the steps to a tee. Jesus was doing the exact same thing as Audi except his rocks started out much bigger and after cutting them down and bagging them up they were the size of Audi's two large white rock. That's when I knew Jesus was a big time dealer, much bigger than Audi. I didn't know the cash value of what either of them had, but I knew from the time Audi had started selling he had been making some type of profit. He had bought himself a car, and a new gold chain with a diamond crusted cross pendant. Anytime we were out and he had to pay for something he pulled out a big roll of twenty dollar bills.

Audi pulled the fifth of Hennessy and swisher sweet from the brown paper bag. He tossed the cigar over to Jose who was already in the process of breaking down a big bud of weed. Audi filled two styrofoam cups with ice cubes, Hennessy and Coke. He gave me the one with more Coke and less

Hennessy. Marcos mother came inside and I could tell she knew the kitchen area was off limit due to job Jesus was currently doing. She signaled for Jesus to go outside but he didn't want to leave all his work unattended so he gave Audi a nod to go and make the transaction. When Audi returned he had two twenty dollar bills bald up in one hand and his sack filled with the white stones in the other. He stuffed the forty dollars inside his front pants pocket then pulled one of the white rocks from the bag, chipping a piece from it and handing it over to Marcos mother who took it and ran towards her bedroom. I wasn't a loud mouth girl, the type that always had to be heard and butting into her boyfriend and his friends conversations. I was more quiet and observant especially around folks I didn't know that well. Mama would always say don't be the one that talk so much, because you will hear nothing. As I got older I started to understand more of what mama meant by that. Jose fired up one end of the blunt and started puffing out clouds of smoke. He passed it to Audi who dragged it a few times then handed it over to me. After I took my turn of puffs I walked over to the kitchen area and handed it off to Jesus who was still cutting up rocks. He held the blunt between his lips, inhaling the smoke first then exhaling it from his nose. He repeated the motion like three times as he continued cutting and bagging the rocks. After two more hard pulls from the blunt he inhaled the smoke holding it in a little longer than before then like a ragging bull he exhaled two heavy clouds of smoke from his nostrils. He pulled the blunt from between his lips trying not to get residue from the cocaine on it. Marcos mother returned from her bedroom just as Jesus had finished his work in the kitchen so it was no longer off limits to her. She started going through the cabinets, unintentionally slamming each one as she closed it. "What the hell you looking for" Marcos yelled

His mother didn't have a direct response to him, but instead mumbled a few sentences to herself as she kept up her search for whatever it was she was missing.

"Man she tweaking" Jose said casually while brushing off the fact that she really was. I had been around drug addicts before, hell I had a few family members who were, but I had never been around someone right after they had hit their stuff. I tried not to stare as she rumble through the cabinets and drawers one by one finding things that she wasn't really look for but still at search for what she was hoping she found. *She picked a fine time to go on a hut for a lost item* I thought to myself. After a while I gave up trying to figure her out and started to ignore the fact that she was even there like everyone else had seem to have done a long time ago.

Audi made over three hundred dollars in that one night selling his rocks at Marcos house.

I couldn't believe how many times the same people would come back to buy. At times they had different folks with them, but still that was a lot of crack in such a little time. I knew Marcos mother knew what they all were doing out of her house because she was a user of their product herself, but I wondered if his grandparents who only stayed feet away knew what was going on in their duplex. I didn't see them much, every once in awhile if it was early in the day they would have their front door cracked open just a bit. I'm sure they had to know something living right there in the middle of it.

CHAPTER 30

It didn't take long for Mr. Tate to find out Audi was dealing. Every time he went home he had new expensive things. First it was the car and jewelry, then he had to go and buy new tires and rims. Mr. Tate knew he didn't have a job to pay for all that expensive stuff and I know he knew my little job couldn't cover the cost so there was no other explanation besides drug dealing or stealing and Audi wasn't a thief. He told Audi he was a grown man and old enough to make his own decisions, but there was no way in hell he could live under his roof if he was going to deal drugs. He told him it wasn't his place to tell his mother, that would have to be something she'd have to discover about her boy on her own. *I guess like the abortion he made us have, why couldn't he let him be a grown man and make that choice on his own* I thought to myself. Maybe we wouldn't be here in this type of situation right now, maybe he'd still be away in college or home on a break visiting his daughter. Maybe we'd be living in our own place by now like Tifa and Deuces or maybe we'd be married and planning to move to another state like Audi had mentioned before. Somewhere like Florida were we could walk on the beach and eat at the boardwalk anytime we wanted. I saw pictures of it on a college brochure Audi had received in the mail while he was deciding on which college to attend.

At the time, I thought it was crazy that he had to go all the way to another state just for college, but now thinking back it could have been a good thing.

I flipped through the Apartment Guide folding the corner of the pages for the ones that were in our price range.

I told Audi it was good I hadn't quit my job

like he kept trying to get me to do. The amount of money he was bringing in was more than enough to cover five hundred dollar rent, we just needed some type of proof of income, and that's where I came in. Once I got to the end of the book I went back through to all the pages I had folded and really looked over all the details of the apartments. I narrowed it down to the best six places and shared the choices with Audi. I phoned each of their leasing offices to see if they had any one bedroom apartments available, all but two had some ready to rent. It was almost five o'clock in the evening on a Saturday and all the leasing offices were getting ready to close and wouldn't open back up until Monday. They all gave me a list of items I would need to lease their apartment. The ones that were asking for too much extra stuff I crossed off the list. Audi and I were excited about getting a place together, that's all we talked about that night. I got lost in the photos from the

Apartment Guild, Imaging each unit as my own. Picturing how each room would look in my mind. From the living room, to the kitchen, kitchen to the bedroom and bedroom to the bathroom I had a detailed vision of what everything would look like. With all the stuff in Audi's bedroom and all the stuff from my bedroom, we had enough to get us started. We decided my television would go in our bedroom and his would go in the living room since it was larger. I hadn't told mama yet, I wanted to wait until it was written in stone, but I'm sure once I did tell her she would happily box up some of her old household items to give us. Audi joked that I would now have to clean, wash clothes and cook dinner every night in our new place. I laughed as he continued to add things that I would be responsible for doing to his list. I created a verbal list of my own for him. We both died in laughter as our lists kept growing, trying to out do one another. He stood up hovering over me, wrapping each hand around my wrists and pulling me up from the bed into his arms. My head resting on his chest, I could feel the slow steady beat of his heart in my ear. Our bodies felt connected like a magnet to medal. Our heartbeats had become in sync. The energy flow from our bodies did all the talking as we stood there holding on to each in silence. With all the bad things that had happened up to that point, I started to feel like some good was about to come, and the feeling put a smile on my face.

CHAPTER 31

I hadn't heard from Audi at all that day. It was close to midnight and each time I dialed his number all I got was a continuous ring before sending me to voicemail.

" I know he can hear the dam phone" I said angrily,

hanging up for about the twentieth time then dialing the digits again. After another failure to answer I left a message.

"You so out of line, why the hell you not answering the phone.

You know we have to go look at apartments in the morning and you just not going to answer or call back"

I yelled through the receiver before hanging up and dialing back again.

"Please Audi….

Just call me back. If you've done something

that you know I'm going to be mad about I promise I don't care just call me and we can talk about it"
I pleaded to his voicemail.
I thought of every reason why he wouldn't call or answer his phone and I prayed that he hadn't cheated on me again and if he had he just needed to be a man and own up to it. Instead of trying to hide behind it. That was the only explanation I could think of as to why he wouldn't want to talk to me.
But why not just turn the phone off I thought to myself.
Staring at the ceiling with what started as anger quickly turned into heartbreak.
I hated being lied too.
He had promised he would be there to pick me up. We planned out the whole day and the day was now gone and it was slipping into the early morning.
How could he,
how could he do me like this,
just when I thought I had shed enough tears

and had felt enough heartache,
here is was,
back again,
taking over my body and soul.
I didn't want to believe it, that he could
really break my heart again especially after
the conversation we had just had the night
before. We both expressed how excited we
were to be getting our own place, own rules
and possibly starting our on family for a
second time.
My mind kept telling me I was a fool and
my sweet Audi wasn't the same Audi,
maybe he had a change of heart and just
didn't know how to break it to me. Or
maybe he knew I wasn't the same old Fre
and there was no way he could see himself
dealing with the new Fre.
I just couldn't let my heart believe it though,
that he would just desert me. Not my Audi,
that was just not like him.

CHAPTER 32

Opening my eyes,
I thought back to the last thing I
remembered doing just a few hours prior.
My head felt weighed down as I slowly
lifted my body from the bed. I realized I had
cried myself to sleep and it caused me to
wake up with a migraine headache.
Checking my voicemail to see if I had slept
through a call from Audi, but was instead
greeted with a recording letting me know I
had no new messages. A sharp pain shot
through my head and made its way down to
my heart before resting in my stomach. I
instantly felt sick. Running to the bathroom I
sat on the toilet and cried my eyes out.
The feeling of butterflies filled my gut,
it was a kind I had never felt before,
they even felt broken,

sitting at the pit of my stomach unable to fly. It felt like they too were dying inside me.

I began to cry out for God to help me, I didn't know exactly what I needed help with I just knew I needed him.

The phone began to ring and I ran to it as fast as I could.

"Hello" I said with suspense

Hoping it was Audi's voice that would respond.

"Umm... Hey Fre hunny,

how you doing,

This Mr.T" he said before taking a long pause.

Ok… I though to myself wonder why he was calling me when I hadn't heard shit from his son in almost two days.

"Baby I hate to call you like this" he said with another long pause that started me to worry.

"Come on and say what the hell you gotta say man,

where the hell is Audi and why he got you

calling my phone. Is he ok, is he in the hospital or even possibly in jail" I thought. That could sure explain why he wasn't answering my calls. I felt a slight bit of joy start to come over my body, but then he asked if I was sitting down.

"Why, why would it matter" I thought as the feeling of joy immediately turned into a feeling of fear and the butterflies I thought had died were back up and active and taking over my entire body.

"NOOO….!
Please Mr. Tate,
No no no no, I can't,
Whyyy….. Lord why" I screamed so loud making mama run into my room screaming. "Girl what's yo problem in here" mama yelled.

Studying the lifeless look on my face covered with tears, she grabbed me and pulled me into her arm, with fright on her face she pulled the phone receiver that was still glued to my ear and spoke into it.

"Who is this" she asked through the phone. Closely listening to every word spoken from Mr. Tates mouth, she fell to her knees speechless.
"My God…, I'm so sorry" she cried.

CHAPTER 33

God takes the ones he needs the most, at least that's what I kept hearing. So I guess everybody I needed God needed more. Reminded me of that stupid saying mama always said, *everything happens for a reason.*

I was about tired of hearing all of them. No matter how bad the tragedy, somebody was going to make it Gods doing. A innocent boy gets shot, a baby dies at the hands of a abusive parent, a grandmother dies of cancer and it's all Gods doing, he needed them in a better place. Well maybe it was getting close to my time to go to this better place. I just couldn't see him taking everything I love and just leaving me here. What kind of God would that be, to

leave me behind. He's so merciful, but I felt no mercy. It felt like deja vu I was reliving the pain that I had already felt before. The type of pain that had no cure, it would ease up just a little, make you think it might have left, and before you knew it, it would reappear and remind you that it hadn't gone anywhere, it was there to stay forever.
My heart was shattered and nothing or no one could repair it. Just the thought of someone trying made me nauseous.
The depression that clouded over my body was nothing like the last time, it was ten times worse, I never imagined having to grieve the loss of two loves. What had I done to deserve such extreme punishment.
I would never know the answer,
like so many other questions that I had that were still being deprived of a simple explanation.
Love, joy and happiness is not meant for me and now I understand that.
I just wish I knew it before falling in love,

I guess everything happens for a reason.

REASONS
II
The Love Prize

Five year's later……

I tossed the towel on his chest for him to cleanup the semen he had ejaculated out of his rock hard penis.
Standing in front of the floor length mirror I adjusted my bra before slipping my house dress over my body. I cleared the ash from the blunt then replaced it back in between my lips. I Brushed my hair into place and wrapping a rubber band around it to make a low ponytail. Clearing the ash once again

from the blunt I passed it to Mister who was taking his sweet time putting back on his clothes. He would never act right and do like I wanted him too. Get dress and get out. He was becoming too needy, breaking all the rules and I just couldn't have that anymore. He act as if he couldn't comprehend that I was not looking for anything but a little pleasure once in awhile. I had promised myself long ago that I would never love again. I had a mental restraining order on love and it had to stay fifty feet away, but just like an ex it kept trying to get close to me. I had my heart on lockdown, it wasn't just closed for repairs and would open back up soon,

no,

it was closed for good.

After all the loves I had lost, I knew better not to let another slip in. I was content with being alone forever, although it wasn't a choice that I had clearly made on my own, it was just the way it had to be.

What else did he want from me, he had a
key to the box, but he needed more he
wanted the key to my heart. What he didn't
know was that key had been broken inside
its lock and it would take a love surgeon to
pry it out.

Made in the USA
San Bernardino, CA
30 June 2018